# ALSO BY TERENCE FAHERTY

Tales of the Star Republic

The Quiet Woman

*The Owen Keane Mysteries*

Deadstick
Live to Regret
The Lost Keats
Die Dreaming
Prove the Nameless
The Ordained
Orion Rising
Eastward in Eden
The Confessions of Owen Keane

*The Scott Elliott Mysteries*

Kill Me Again
Come Back Dead
Raise the Devil
Dance in the Dark
The Hollywood Op

# FILES OF THE STAR REPUBLIC

# FILES OF THE
# STAR REPUBLIC

TERENCE FAHERTY

THE GISBOURNE PRESS

Cover: Cover Story Design

Interior Design: Sue Trowbridge, interbridge.com

Author Photo: Paul Chaffee

This book is a work of fiction and the persons and places and institutions described herein are imaginary or used fictitiously. Any resemblance to actual persons or places or institutions is entirely coincidental.

Print ISBN: 978-0-692-91141-9

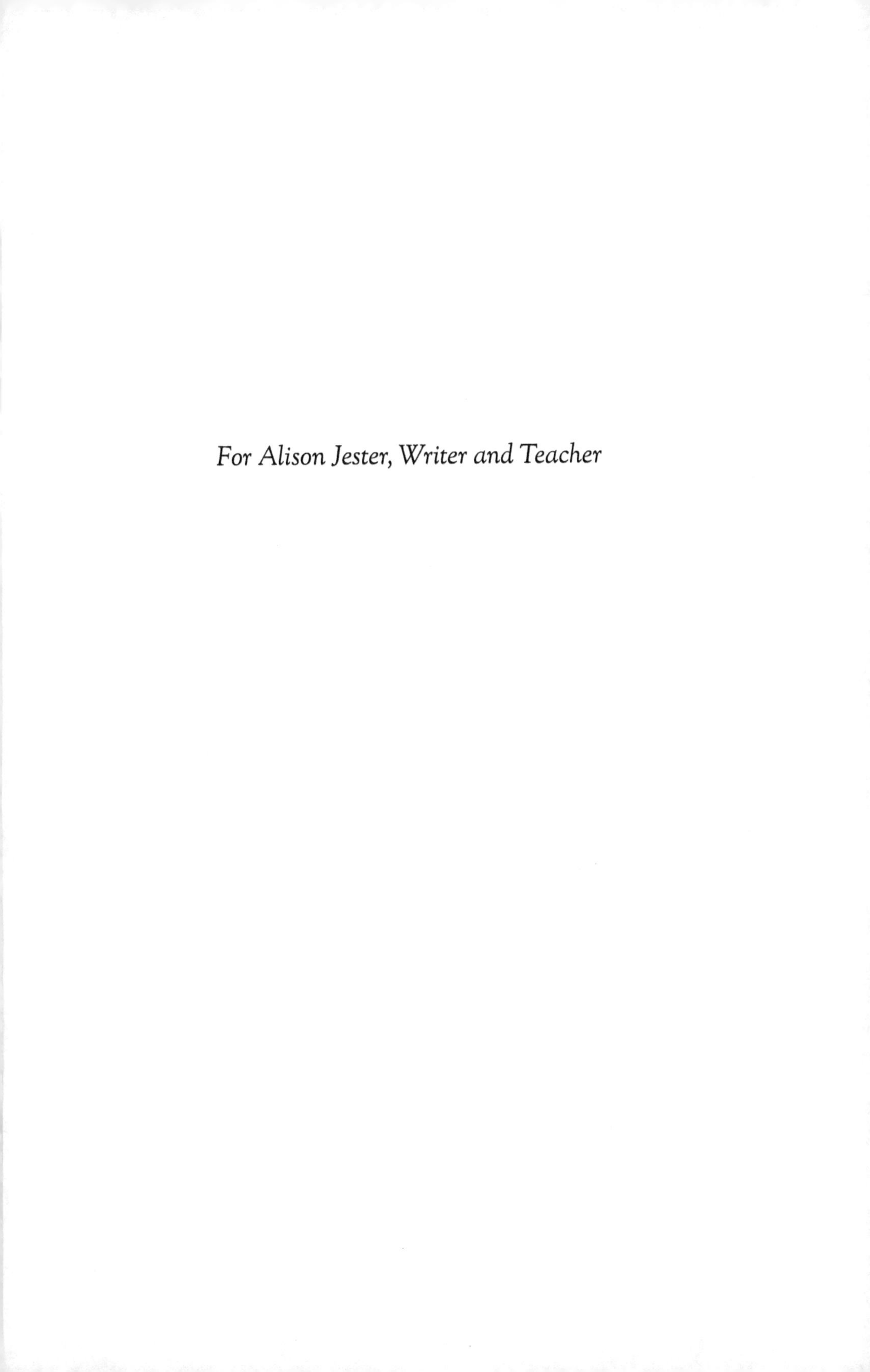

*For Alison Jester, Writer and Teacher*

# Contents

# Acknowledgements

"Goodnight, Dr. Kobel" first appeared in *Indiannual 4*, Writers' Center of Indianapolis, 1988; "Into Legend" first appeared in *Indiannual 5*, Writers' Center of Indianapolis, 1990; "Back Home Again" first appeared in *The Flying Island*, Writers' Center of Indianapolis, Summer 1993; "Where Is He Now?" first appeared in *Ellery Queen Mystery Magazine*, February 2005; "Infinite Uticas" first appeared in *Ellery Queen Mystery Magazine*, June 2017. The remaining stories are published here for the first time.

# Introduction

This is the second volume of tales I collected during my four-decade career with Indiana's newspaper of record, the *Indianapolis Star Republic*. None of the stories that follow actually became part of the paper's official record, because none appeared in the *Star Republic*'s pages. They were too paranormal, too peculiar, or just too private to be served up to the citizens of Indianapolis with their orange juice and oatmeal. But they all meant something to me.

I was slow to spot that the most important stories of my journalistic career would be the ones I couldn't get past my editor. At first, I went after what my coworkers called "nut stories" because I thought they would be high profile. Like many another cub reporter, my earliest ambition was simply to get my byline printed as often as possible. Then, too, because most of what a beginner gets to work on is routine, formula copy, I was attracted by the twisted quality of these stories and by the challenge of telling them right.

Even after I'd recognized the career limitations that came

with the nut story specialty—not only that much of my best work would not see print, but also the tendency of people to consider the specialist in weird tales weird himself—I stuck with it. I'd become seduced by then by the stories and by the odd idea that what I was collecting weren't individual strange tales but fragments of a single larger story, clues to a larger mystery. You could call that mystery the human condition if you'd like, though even that grand title doesn't do justice to my earliest ambitions.

You might be thinking that Indianapolis, Indiana, was a strange place in which to look for the secrets of the universe. I worried about that myself, around the time my interest in nut stories became a passion. Though I was born and raised in Indianapolis, I'd long thought of the city as a place I'd one day leave behind.

My dismissive attitude was reflected in a line from one of my first published articles: "Indianapolis is a city built on the banks, at the foot, and in the shadow of nothing very special." As a statement of geography, that unkind remark was more or less correct. The location of Indianapolis, at the center of its state, was a political compromise that reflected the growing dominance of the northern counties over the earlier-settled Ohio River Valley. The result for the city has been a certain flavorless quality, a lack of a well-defined character that's at the heart of both the city's traditionally low self-esteem and its recent renaissance.

It's ironic but true that over the course of my career, while many more distinctive northern cities withered, Indianapolis blossomed, and for many of the same reasons for which it used to be derided. For example, the absence of a dominant industry protected it during economic downturns. And the blandness of the city's geography meant that there were no natural boundaries to keep it from sending its tax base sprawling in all directions. Most important, the blank-slate quality of the city's character allowed its leader-of-the-moment to write his or her vision of the future in a bold hand.

But long before Indy's renaissance, I'd changed my mind about the city. I'd come to value it—and the entire state of Indiana—for reasons that had nothing to do with tax rates or political programs. I'd recognized it as the perfect place for a researcher of the unusual to work.

That statement might seem to have its neck stretched and waiting for the ax of contradiction. It might be argued, for example, that more strange things happen in Los Angeles in a day than the entire state of Indiana sees in a year. I would reply that the profusion of the weird in LA is more of a hindrance than a help. Researching the unusual in Los Angeles or New York makes no more sense than listening at a cataract for the sound of a single drop. The big-small-town atmosphere of Indianapolis offers the proper compromise between peace and noise, with enough lonely moments to allow the tinder of solitary thought to accumulate and enough human collisions to send off random sparks. And, to return to a water image, Indy's bland, ordinary face is a still pond on which the tiniest pebble sends out clear ripples. For that was the nature of the stories I was after. They were ripples, echoes, whispers that would not be spoken in an empty place and not heard in a crowded one.

As to my naïve certainty that I would be able to piece these stories together into a meaningful whole, that heady moment was followed by a long period of wondering whether I would. More recently, I've admitted to myself that the single, unifying story will probably never come. The most I really hope for now is that I will continue to find signs, no more blatant than broken twigs and bent blades of grass, indicators that there are good reasons to keep asking the little questions, even if there is no hope of a big answer.

# WHERE IS HE NOW?

---

Most premonition stories are about as newsworthy as a hot tip on last week's stock market. Let a boat sink or a plane crash and any number of people will call the nearest newspaper to report vague feelings or signs or dream warnings from Aunt Lucille that kept them from boarding. Few if any think to call when the information would actually be useful.

Walter Ashby didn't call the *Star Republic*, the Indianapolis paper for which I labor, to report premonitions of his approaching death. But when rumors of them began to circulate shortly after Ashby's obituary appeared, they so intrigued E.N. Boxleiter, my editor, that he asked me to look into it. Ashby hadn't actually spotted his end coming, as it turned out, but it seemed he knew who would be holding his left hand when Death seized his right.

My initial contact was the source of the intriguing rumor,

a woman name Clarice O'Connor. She was a third-generation mortician whose family's business occupied a pseudo antebellum mansion in Broad Ripple, a neighborhood on the north side of Indy. At one time, the home might have had acres of manicured lawn as its setting. Now it was squeezed between a muffler shop and a consignment art gallery. A little of the old gentility survived inside the building, which looked like it had been furnished exclusively from maiden-aunt estate sales. O'Connor's office had a modern, businesslike desk, but the piece of furniture she waved me to was nothing less than a settee, with a doily on each arm.

O'Connor herself was short and ruddy-cheeked, with a friendliness that remained even after I'd identified myself as a non-bereaved.

"I feel like I work for the *Star Republic* myself," she began. "I talk to you people almost every day. Call in obituaries, you know, after I've interviewed the family. Not that the widow, Joyce Ashby, mentioned anything supernatural when I spoke with her. She just gave me the standard stuff, the deceased's age: fifty-one, profession: teacher, survivors: her. But at the viewing everybody was talking about it. Especially after Barry Clarkson himself walked in.

"You might remember him as Clark Clarkson. That's the professional name he used when he was a disc jockey at WIBC back in the sixties. And Clark Clarkson is the name the dear departed—Walter Ashby, I mean—started asking everybody about a week or so before he died.

"The guy who told me about it is another teacher at Walter's school. According to this guy, Walter just came in one day and asked him if he remembered an Indy DJ named Clark Clarkson who introduced a lot of the early stuff of the Beatles and the Stones. It was a trivia question, you know, like 'Whatever happened to what's-his-name?' Walter said he'd just gotten up that morning with Clarkson's name in his head. He'd asked his wife about him, which she later confirmed at the viewing, though she really didn't want to talk about it.

"Anyway, over the course of the next few days Walter asked several other teachers at the school—ones of the right vintage—if they remembered Clarkson and knew what had become of him. It's funny when you think about it. When we were kids, those DJs were our big celebrities, but a lot of them were barely older than we were, and I'll bet none of them made much more than minimum wage."

Salaries being an uncomfortable subject for a journalist, I nudged us back to the point by asking what had happened next to the nostalgic Walter Ashby.

"What happened next," O'Connor said, "was the punch line, for Walter and the story. He's out walking one night—he was a big walker, one of those guys who pumps his arms and wiggles his hips like he's in the Olympics—and he has a heart attack. Bang, drops right down on the edge of the street. This was in Williams Creek, a neighborhood just north of here. Nice older homes.

"The guy in the nearest house comes out to help. He can't revive Walter, so he calls for an ambulance on his cell phone and stays with Walter till it gets there. The ambulance rushes Walter to St. Vincent's, but it's too late, he's dead.

"Meanwhile, the cops are making out a report and they get the name of the Good Samaritan, the guy who tried to help Walter. It's Barry Clarkson, formerly Clark Clarkson, the guy Walter's been asking everybody about. Do you believe it? It's like Walter had a vision of his own death, of the last face he'd see."

It had been a very incomplete vision, as it hadn't included Ashby clutching at his own chest. But that omission didn't spoil it for O'Connor.

"So that's the story that was flying around the Gardenia Room on the night of Walter Ashby's showing. But then it got better. The viewing was scheduled to run from seven till nine, and who should walk in at eight-thirty but Barry Clarkson. A couple of people recognized him even though he's changed a lot—no beard now and gray in his hair—and a hush fell over the room. You know it's gotten seriously silent when you can notice a drop in the volume of a Midwestern wake, given how polite most of them are to begin with.

"I was greeting people that night on behalf of O'Connor's, so I stepped up and introduced myself. Barry was *so* sweet.

And that voice. You could almost imagine that it was 1965 again and he was announcing that 'Downtown' was the number one song for the third week in a row.

"Somehow Barry had heard the story of Walter's premonition. And he'd made the effort to come and meet Mrs. Ashby. So I introduced them. And that was *the* moment. Joyce was so touched. And you could see this bond forming right away. I remember thinking, maybe Walter's premonition wasn't really about who was going to be with him when he died. Maybe it was about who Joyce was going to be with after he was gone. Maybe, without really knowing it, he was arranging for someone to take care of her."

To paraphrase O'Connor, you know it's gotten seriously sentimental when a mortician is touched, given the heavy doses of emotion they're exposed to daily. And she was touched. She glanced at the box of tissues reserved for her customers but didn't reach for it. I didn't either. I asked instead for Mrs. Ashby's address and the name of the teacher who had first told O'Connor the story.

I tracked down the teacher first, catching him between classes at a noisy Broad Ripple middle school. His name was Burris, and he confirmed everything that O'Connor had told me and did it with a breathlessness that made the lady mortician seem like a cynic. But he also added one piece to the puzzle. As he backed into a classroom that sounded like it was full of warring cats, he admitted that he was the one who had called Barry Clarkson to tell him of Walter Ashby's premonition.

"I thought it was important for him to know," Burris said. And then, with a catch in his voice, "I thought Walter would have wanted him to know."

It was shaping up to be an interesting piece. All I needed to cap it off would be a quote from the widow and one from Barry "Clark" Clarkson. I thought about trying to get the two together, to check for signs of the bonding Clarice O'Connor had spotted, but Clarkson didn't answer his phone.

Joyce Ashby did, but when I mentioned my business she asked for time to think it over. I gave her the hour it took me to have lunch at an ersatz English pub on Westfield Boulevard. When I called her back her using the pub's authentic English phone box, she agreed to talk with me in her home on Gladden, a quiet street off busy Meridian.

Ashby, a slender woman with olive skin and drooping features, was younger than her late husband by about ten years, I estimated, which made her very young to be an overnight widow. The continuing shock of that might have accounted for the vague, distracted way in which she greeted me and listened to my retelling of the story that had thrilled the Gardenia Room. She focused somewhat when I got to Clarkson's entrance at the wake. Focused and brightened.

"Wasn't that the nicest thing? That he should make that effort when, really, there was no connection between him and Walter. Except Walter's death. I guess anybody who tried to help a dying man might stop by his viewing or funeral. But still, it was very nice."

I asked if she wasn't forgetting another connection between the two men. Namely, her husband's sudden interest in Clarkson just days before his death.

"That's just a coincidence," Ashby said. "I mean, what else could it be? It's just a Ripley's Believe It Or Not, which I really hate for Walter's sake. He had a real sense of, ah, dignity, I guess you'd say."

She turned to look at a framed studio portrait of a man with a large, put-upon nose and a seventies moustache, stubbornly maintained. The late Walter Ashby.

"The kids at his school teased him for it, the dignity, but that never seemed to bother him. It didn't bother him when people would honk their horns at him when he was doing the funny speed walking he took up when his doctor told him to exercise. For his heart. But I think this might have bothered him, to be remembered as a Ripley's, an oddity. I think he expected a more dignified epitaph than that."

I asked her if she would prefer that we drop the story, and she did an abrupt about-face.

"Oh no. I can understand people's interest in it. And it may be important to Mr. Clarkson. He might like having his name in the paper again, even for something odd. Maybe it will even help his career. If he still has a career. It couldn't hurt Walter. Could it?"

The question was outside my professional expertise. So I thanked her and left.

Barry Clarkson still wasn't answering his phone, but I drove to the address I'd found with his number in the phone book. I was so close to the end of the story as I then saw it that I was reluctant to let go. O'Connor had described Clarkson's neighborhood as an area of nice, older homes, and that was no more than doing it justice. The former DJ's was a one-story of painted brick on a hillside given over to large rocks and ivy. I could describe his doorbell in detail, too, since I stood pressing it for some time without result.

As I descended the hill to my parked car, I noticed a woman gardening in the next yard. That is to say, I noticed her pretending to garden as she watched me. I forgot about my car and joined her in the daylily bed, introducing myself with my press card, which was my habit with old ladies and policemen.

"You're here about the man who died in the street you say?" she asked, removing one rubber glove so she could scratch at her silver hair. "That was terrible. I've been kicking myself for not going out and asking him what he wanted, that night or one of the others. Or calling the neighborhood patrol to come and talk with him."

I asked if she meant she'd seen Ashby walking through the neighborhood prior to the night he died.

"Walking? I suppose he walked. I never saw a car. But it was him standing there got my attention.

I repeated "standing there" as a question.

"Certainly. Two or three nights in a row. Three nights, I'd say, counting the last one. He'd be standing there in the street staring up at Barry's house for maybe ten minutes at a time, standing very stiff like, not moving. I should have called the patrol but—oh, there's Barry now. Alone for once."

She smiled broadly and waved, and I turned in time to see a light blue Porsche turn into the neighboring drive. I thanked the neighborhood watch committee and hurried back up the hill.

Clarkson must have seen me coming. He was waiting at the top of his drive and he was irritated, his look that of a man forced to deal with a telemarketer when he has both eggs out of the pan and the toast buttered. He was dressed for lunch at a country club and very well preserved for a celebrity whose moment had come and gone thirty years earlier: tall and flat-bellied with thick, slightly long hair that was only graying at the temples or only being allowed to gray there.

He also had, as it turned out, what success manuals called a "winning smile." He flashed it when I drew close enough to mention my business.

"Oh that," he said. "Come on in. When I saw you talking with Mrs. Gorman, I thought you were selling door-to-door. Nice lady, Mrs. Gorman, but she's not all there anymore. Alzheimer's or something. Real shame."

He showed me to a study on the back of the house that contained mementos from his career, the part Walter Ashby had remembered and the long years since. The glory days were represented by old photos, including one showing Clarkson with the Beatles during their 1964 appearance at the Indiana State Fair. For his post-disc-jockey career, there were awards and framed letters of appreciation from a variety of professional organizations and private companies.

"For my voice-overs," Clarkson said. "That's what I've been doing since I sold out in the seventies. Educational films, promotional films. *Better Living though Soybeans*, that kind of stuff. Or *American Widget, the First Hundred Years*. Money's good, but it's very low profile. Nothing like the night I met John, Paul, George, and Ringo out at the fairgrounds. I was somebody that night, let me tell you. Ten thousand screaming virgins in the place, and I could have taken any one of them home. I did take one or two, if memory serves."

Before his memory could serve up dessert, I interrupted to suggest that he might get a moment of his old fame back, courtesy of a dead speed walker.

"Yeah. That was wild, wasn't it? I mean, what are the odds of that happening? I half went to that viewing just to find out if the guy who'd phoned me had been pulling my leg. But the widow herself backed him up.

"She was very nice. Joyce. She seemed so touched by a

little thing like me showing up. My heart really went out to her."

When I asked how he happened to notice her husband in front of his house in the first place, he shrugged. "Just glanced out my front window, and there he was, bent over with his hands on his knees. I would have gone back to whatever I'd been doing, but right then he just sort of tipped over. Didn't put a hand out to soften the fall or anything, which scared the hell out of me. I had nine-one-one punched into my cell phone before I even got down there, not that it did him any good. He was already gone, I think. Never said a word, never opened his eyes."

Just to get his reaction, I mentioned Gorman's observation that Ashby had stood there looking up at the painted brick house for ten minutes or more.

"Did she say that?" Clarkson asked. For the first time, I noticed a smoothness in his baritone that reminded me of his profession. "Really? I'd hate to think he had that much warning and didn't ring somebody's bell. I certainly would have gone down to speak to him if I'd noticed him sooner.

"Then again, Mrs. G might be remembering somebody else or just making it up. Like I said before, she's not always in the here and now. For example, the night it all happened she told me she'd seen the same man in the neighborhood three nights running. But nobody else saw that. And Joyce told me her husband never took the same route two nights in a row."

Clarkson had looked at his watch several times during that speech. I took the hint and got to my feet, asking if he'd mind being photographed for the article. He handed me a black-and-white publicity shot that might have been taken that morning.

At the door, he said, "Don't feel like you have to make a big deal out of this for my sake. I turn down half of the things my agent sends me as it is. And it's not like I saved the guy's life."

I walked down to my car, but only to deposit the glossy photograph. Clarkson's neighbor was still spading the dirt around her lilies. I headed her way.

"Still here?" Gorman asked when she noticed me, which suggested that her short-term memory was doing better than advertised.

I apologized for bothering her a second time, reminding her that our first chat had been interrupted by Clarkson's arrival. Then I asked her about the comment she'd made when Clarkson had pulled in. That he was "alone for once."

She had a glove off again and was scratching away vigorously at her silver crown. "I didn't mean anything by that. Not really. Barry's a ladies' man, that's all. Always has been. There's always a steady stream of them over there. Blondes mostly. Wouldn't have guessed there were that many blondes in Indiana. We've been waiting for twenty years for that stream to dry up, but it hasn't, so we all just joke about it.

"It does seem to be running a little slower though, that stream of women. The latest girlfriend's being coming over for a solid month. For Barry, that's like making it to your golden anniversary."

I asked if she was a blonde.

"No, that's another change. She's dark, with pretty Mediterranean skin. Quite the Mona Lisa."

As it happened, I'd met a woman that day who matched that description: Joyce Ashby. I decided another talk with her was in order, but when I neared my car, Barry Clarkson came down his drive and placed himself between me and the Chevy's door.

"You've figured it all out, haven't you? I knew you had when you went back to talk with that old busybody. Come up to the house so we can talk."

I declined the invitation, feeling more comfortable under Gorman's very watchful gaze.

"I'm not threatening you," Clarkson said. "I'm not crazy. I just want you to hear our side of it. I've called Joyce and asked her to come over. You can at least hear us out. We didn't hurt Walter, not deliberately. And we certainly didn't murder him. You can check with his doctors on that. He killed himself. He got himself worked up, and his bum heart gave out.

"All Joyce and I did was fall in love. You don't need to know where or when; that's not the issue. Somehow, Walter found out. We don't know how. He wouldn't come right out and confront Joyce with it. He hated anything like an argument. He just asked her one day if she remembered Clark Clarkson, just to let her know, like just the mention of my old name would scare her back to the straight and narrow. When that didn't work, he started coming by here. At least that's how we pieced it together after Mrs. Gorman started gossiping the night Walter died. He came three nights in a row but couldn't bring himself to knock on my door and confront me. I didn't notice him till that last night, I swear it. And his heart was already seizing up, just like I told you. He had a weak heart. Ask anybody who knew him. Ask Joyce when she gets here."

Clarkson's mention of the widow reminded me of a point that wanted clearing up. I told him I'd given Joyce a chance to kill the story and she'd passed on it. Why had she let in the daylight if she had an illicit affair to cover up?

"That was my fault," Clarkson said. "I talked her into it. I figured the more people heard that story the better it would be for us. When I first got the call about the premonition business from that guy at Walter's school, I saw it as an opportunity. Joyce and I want to be together as a couple. We're tired of sneaking around. Walter's dying was a terrible thing, but it was also our chance. Or it would have been, if he hadn't dropped dead right in front of my house. That screwed us but good. I mean, how would it look if we suddenly started seeing one another? No one would accept Walter's dying on my doorstep as a coincidence. The Mrs.

Gorman Network would have been staying with that story twenty-four hours a day.

"Then I heard that Walter had been asking his friends about me. I figure he was just after my address, but the friends thought his interest was some kind of message from the spirit world. And I saw that as the perfect solution for Joyce and me. I could go to the viewing. I could be this consoling stranger that Joyce meets next to her husband's coffin. Meets through her husband's intercession, in a way."

It was the happy ending Clarice O'Connor had given the story. As Joyce Ashby pulled up and joined Clarkson in a tentative embrace, I wondered if the couple realized that their choice of a cover story would ensure that Walter and his strange death would always be with them, a memento trotted out by well-meaning friends at every anniversary. And I wondered how long it would be before they grew to hate the mention of it. I wondered, too, seeing as we were more or less standing on the very spot, whether the dying Walter had recognized Clarkson in his last seconds and been consoled by the idea that his wife, however unfaithful, would have a shoulder to cry on.

Clarkson hadn't pulled out that stop, hadn't claimed that he'd received some kind of deathbed blessing from the man he'd wronged. If he had, I might have blown the story wide open, fairy tale or no fairy tale.

As it was, I wished the couple luck and called it a day.

# GOODNIGHT, DR. KOBEL

Economically speaking, the southwestern suburbs of Indianapolis were undiscovered country for quite a while. Growing up, I thought of them as a stretch of truck farms and nurseries and not much else. While the area's still not Chicago at noon, it has profited greatly from Indy's recent growth. New families and businesses have moved in, bringing more cars than the roads can handle and more kids than the schools can handle. One business might have brought in something it couldn't handle itself. A ghost, to be exact.

The business was a restaurant and bar built in an old sawmill and called the Indiana Lumber Company. Shortly after it opened, the vandalism began. The help would lock the place up at night, swept and tidy, and return the next day to find bottles broken and tables overturned. There was never any sign of a forced entry. Four occurrences in two months had left the police baffled.

The restaurant's owner, Roger Hartman, called the story in to Indy's daily newspaper, the *Star Republic*. E.N. Boxleiter, my editor, sent me to check out Hartman's report and Hartman himself.

"If it starts to sound like free publicity, refer him to the ad department," Boxleiter told me.

From the outside, there wasn't much to distinguish the Indiana Lumber Company from the other small businesses along Bluff Road. "Bar and Restaurant" appeared in small print on the modest sign at the edge of the gravel parking lot, but there didn't appear to have been a lot of exterior renovation done to the gray building, which was narrow at the Bluff end but long. The interior of the place was a pleasant surprise. The rough plank walls and railings contributed to the sawmill conceit and gave the dining area the appropriate smell of freshly sawn wood. It was divided into different levels under a high ceiling with exposed beams. A long bar, built of cedar and backed by an impressive collection of bottles, ran along one wall. That wall and the other three were decorated with the kind of memorabilia common in casual restaurants. Movie posters and neon signs from dead businesses shared the space with old tools and a few paintings.

Roger Hartman was a short man in his forties who carried much of his weight in a paunch supported by a belt and suspenders. He wore cowboy boots with upturned, pointed toes. The bottom of his head was covered by a black beard and the top by a few strands of slick hair, carefully arranged. His large eyes were as brown as a cow's and nearly as guileless, which put me on my guard.

"Felt like talking to somebody in the media about this," he said as we shook hands. "Felt like I needed more heads working on it. Maybe if a lot of people read about it, somebody will think of something."

As we sat down at the bar, I complimented him on his restaurant.

"Thanks," he said. "Did all the decorating myself. Everything's out of second-hand shops, except for a couple of pictures my wife did." He indicated an oil painting that hung behind the bar. It showed a perfectly flat horse standing in a perfectly flat field.

"Down there's my pride and joy," he said, pointing to one of the room's end walls. The decorations there were dominated by a life-size portrait of a serious-looking man seated in a dark office. The painting hung just beneath the rafters.

"Set me back a bit, but it was worth it. I always liked FDR, so it caught my eye right away. The more I looked at it, the more I liked it. Thought it would give the place a little class. Funny thing is, some of my customers tell me it isn't Roosevelt."

It wasn't. The shape of the head was about right, and so

was the gray hair, but the resemblance to Franklin Roosevelt ended with the old fashioned "pince-nez" glasses the gentleman wore high on his nose. The sitter's chin was no match for the president's, and the high, stiff collar he wore suggested an earlier administration.

"Anyway," Hartman said, "I like it and I intend it keep it, if I can stay in business. We opened three months ago. The trade was good from the start. Not super, but steady. We get a pretty good lunchtime crowd and happy hour. Weeknights are slow, but we have a band in on the weekend and things really pick up.

"The disturbances started one week after we opened. John, that's my bartender over there"—Hartman indicated a young man with dark hair and a beard very like Hartman's own who was polishing glasses at the opposite end of the bar—"locked up that night. I opened the next morning and damn near died. Ten or twelve bottles of liquor were broken around the bar and half the tables were turned over. I called the cops from the pay phone by the front door.

"I want to say before we go any further that the police have done a fine job. They were over here quick that first day and every time since. They went over the doors and windows real careful. There was no sign of a break-in. Never has been. The windows and the dead bolts on the doors were locked. There's no way to lock the windows from the outside, or the dead bolts either without a key.

"It's happened three more times since then, but it isn't

always exactly the same. I had to replace the mirror over the bar after the second time. Last week, all the decorations were off the walls, at least all the ones you can reach. FDR up there or whoever he is wasn't touched.

"As far as we can tell, there's never been a thing taken. There's also never been a note or a crank call or anything to say who's doing it or what they want."

Hartman paused for a moment and played with some change on the bar. When he looked up, he was smiling sheepishly. "I guess there's just one more thing to tell you, but I don't want you to take it wrong. Some of my customers got talking one night and decided that what I had was a poltergeist, you know, a destructive ghost like they had in that movie a few years back. I'm not saying I believe in that stuff, but I try to keep an open mind. I got the name of a professor at the Lockerbie University in town who studies that kind of thing. Smith's his name, Jim Smith. Regular guy. He got all excited when I told him the story. He came by, asked a lot of questions about the place, even went to talk with the people who used to own it when it was a sawmill. He had the idea that somebody might have been killed here in some sort of accident, and that they might still be wandering around.

"Well, anyway, it turned out to be a bust. No one could remember anyone dying here or even getting hurt. Seems like this must have been the safest sawmill ever operated in the state of Indiana. Jim and I stayed here a couple of nights, all locked in with his equipment. We drank a lot of beer, but not enough for us to start seeing ghosts. He said he might try again, but I think he's pretty much given up.

"That's about the whole story. Brand new restaurant, owned and operated by one of the nicest fellows you'd ever want to meet, wrecked for no reason. No sign of a forced entry and no dead lumbermen whooping it up after hours. Got any ideas?"

I thought it over. During Hartman's story, I'd felt someone watching me. I looked up suddenly and met the gaze of John the bartender. It wasn't a friendly gaze. He tried to stare me down, gave it up, and stomped out of the dining room, swinging his towel at the chairs he passed.

I asked Hartman whether his bartender still had a key to the place.

"Now don't you go starting on John," Hartman said. "The police tried that, and we almost came to a parting over it. He's my brother's boy. He's had some troubles, but he's okay now."

John was gone, but I still had the feeling I was being watched. I looked around the room. The only candidate was the old gentleman with the pince-nez glasses hanging on the end wall. He wasn't pleased with me either. I was curious about the painting, and that gave me an idea. I couldn't tell Hartman who was breaking up his place, but I might solve another mystery for him. I asked him where he had purchased the portrait.

"A place called Ackerman's out on East Washington," Hartman said. He took my question to mean our interview was over and extended his hand. "Thanks for coming by. I hope one of your readers will think of something that's gotten past me."

Washington is the most important east-west surface road in Indianapolis, forming with Meridian Street the intersection from which all other streets in the city are numbered. Unlike Meridian, however, Washington has no fine homes to reflect its stature. Heading east from downtown, the street falls on hard times almost immediately. The neighborhoods are made up of old, predominantly frame homes too large for the current owners to both care for and heat. The small businesses reflect the condition of the neighborhoods they front, "used" appearing frequently in their names.

Ackerman's Antiques was one used furniture store surrounded by many and distinguished from the others only by a slight pretension. Most of the offerings in the shop were genuinely old, but they'd been discount pieces when new. Mr. Ackerman was tall and carefully dressed, wearing a Perry Como cardigan with patched elbows and a tie. His skin was pasty and the frames of his glasses were repaired with yellowed tape. He appeared to be a nervous man, and his condition did not improve when I told him that I worked for the *Star Republic* and that I was interested in the portrait he'd sold Roger Hartman.

"Look, buddy," Ackerman said, "I never told him that was a painting of Franklin Delano Roosevelt. He got that idea all by himself." Ackerman smiled unnaturally and adjusted his eyeglasses several times. "I mean, if he thought he was getting a life sized portrait of a president of the United States in oil for peanuts, he wasn't exactly a connoisseur, let me tell you."

I told Ackerman that I wasn't interested in consumer affairs and that Hartman liked his painting, Roosevelt or not. We became fast friends. When I asked him if he knew the identity of the man in the painting, he laughed and shook his head.

"Damned if I do," he said. "I picked it up out in Greenfield at an auction. Some little Baptist Bible college—you know, three buildings and a grove of trees—went belly up, and the bank sold everything but the woodwork. I picked up some nice old office furniture, solid oak some of it, and that picture.

"The name of the place? Let me see. Kobel, I think. Kobel Bible College. I don't think they had much of a football program, let me tell you."

I went back to the office and searched the morgue files for the Kobel Bible College. An hour later I was ready to try another approach. I'd found references in the back issues to another college, the Faith Bible Academy, located just south of the city. I found the college in the current phone book. The president, Dr. Harold Coppin, took my call personally.

"I'm also half the faculty," Dr. Coppin told me. He was familiar with the defunct college in Greenfield and happy to talk with me. When I described the portrait Hartman had acquired, Coppin's response forced the receiver an inch or two from my ear.

"Of course, of course," he said. "I've seen the painting many times. It's a portrait of Dr. Alfred Kobel, the founder of the college. He's been dead now for forty years I would say. No, forty-five. I had the great honor to meet him at the beginning of my ministry. He was a prominent churchman in Indiana and well respected. Dr. Kobel was a leading figure in the Temperance Movement during his early career. At the time I met him, it was all over, of course, but he still spoke of it. The failure of Prohibition was a blow to him, a shadow across his last years."

Dr. Coppin added that he would be proud to accept the portrait as a donation to his school.

I called Roger Hartman to report the results of my research. He took the news that he had one of Indiana's foremost opponents of alcohol hanging in his tavern remarkably well. He was much less patient with Dr. Coppin's suggestion that he give his favorite painting away.

"Not on your life, friend," Hartman said. "Thanks for the tip. I'll be in touch."

Next, I reported to the man who'd given me the assignment. Boxleiter listened to almost half of the story before he told me to forget it. I very nearly had a month later when Roger Hartman called me. Without giving me an explanation, he invited me to dinner at his restaurant. I went that same night.

Hartman came across the room when he saw me, smiling all the way. "Not one broken bottle in a month, thanks to you," he said. He led me to a table, but asked me to look around before sitting down. "Notice anything different?"

The change I'd been expecting had not been made. Dr. Alfred Kobel still hung in his place of honor. The only change I could see was the blonde working behind the bar. I asked if it was John's night off.

Hartman made a face. "Naw, that hothead quit me. Gone off to California and good riddance. That's not what I meant, though. Notice anything else?"

I had to admit that I didn't. Hartman was pleased. He took me by the arm and led me toward Kobel's portrait.

"Your tip on old Alfred was right on the money," Hartman said. "I knew it as soon as I hung up the phone. It had to be his spirit wrecking the place, this den of iniquity he'd suddenly found himself in. But I couldn't bring myself to part with the old guy. Then I got an idea."

He led me to one corner of the room and had me look up at the portrait. From that angle, the light from the ceiling fixtures was reflected by the painting's old varnish, obscuring the image beneath. The glare was uniform, except for a small dull area toward the top. I stepped in front of the portrait to confirm my guess. Kobel's glasses were gone, painted out.

"My wife did a great job, didn't she?" Hartman beamed up at the painting. "Now there's peace in the valley."

# INFINITE UTICAS

On October 15, 1863, the riverboat *Utica*, carrying wounded Union soldiers to the hospitals of Cincinnati, exploded and sank near the Ohio River town of Reynolds, Indiana. Over four hundred passengers and crew died in the accident, which eerily presaged the *Sultana* disaster of 1865 that claimed seventeen hundred lives. The final resting place of the *Utica* remained uncertain until 1989, when a team from the University of Louisville located a wreck in an Indiana cornfield that had formerly been a muddy shoulder of the Ohio. Despite its shattered condition, the buried steamboat was positively identified as the *Utica*.

Eighteen years later, a second expedition was mounted to find the *Utica*. According to the expedition's press release, the 2007 effort was not undertaken because the University of Louisville's claims were incorrect or fraudulent or because any substantial fragment of the steamboat had been missing from the 1989 site. The new search was based on the theory that a second wreck of the exact same ship was buried somewhere under the soil of southern Indiana.

That odd claim caught the attention of E.N. Boxleiter, my editor at an Indianapolis daily, the *Star Republic*. He sent me down to Reynolds to interview the director of SURAS, the Second Utica Research and Archeological Society.

I found the director at the SURAS dig site, also known as the McGregor Farm. Its owner, Hank McGregor, gave me a concise history of the field in question as he drove me to it from the neat farm lot where I'd left my car.

"I wasn't surprised when Dr. Tallion wrote to ask if her group could poke around down there. That section could have been river once. The channel shifts around after floods. That is, the channel used to, before the banks got so built up and paved over. We still lose our bottomland during wet springs. It flooded so bad in 1903, we lost two men with it."

McGregor made the personal connection to that hundred-year-old flood quite naturally, though he was no more than thirty himself. On that mild fall day he was wearing a suit of tan overalls too short at the ankles and wrists and a St. Louis baseball cap.

I asked him how he liked having scientists underfoot.

He repeated the word "scientists," shaking his red-capped head a little. Then he added, "Harvest's done. And this beats working."

We drove through a line of trees and into the field that was prone to flooding. I could see why: Beyond an inadequate-looking levee and another fringe of sycamores, almost leafless and starkly white, was the Ohio River. A line of barges was passing just then, and their loads of coal seemed almost at eye level. At the moment, though, the field was dry enough to support a number of cars and trucks. When we drew up to them, I understood why McGregor had shaken his head at my suggestion that he had scientists underfoot. The vehicles reminded me of the caravans that used to stream into Indianapolis whenever the Grateful Dead came to town. The elderly van we parked next to actually had a bumper sticker that read "American by birth, Deadhead by choice." The people milling around the little encampment were a mixed bunch, some young imitation hippies, some old enough to have been the real thing. A few had been outfitted for a rural adventure by L.L. Bean. Others were dressed like authentic farmhands.

The woman who greeted us officially, Dr. Elizabeth Tallion, looked like she'd dressed for a Casual Friday at some upscale urban office, maybe a bank's. She wore pleated khaki pants, carefully pressed, a crisp white blouse, and—across her shoulders—a lavender sweater. She was a petite woman, perhaps forty, though a schoolgirl's plastic headband held her straight, brown hair away from her broad face. That face was an interesting study. It was fine-featured and unlined, with a small mouth that smiled continuously and dry, brown eyes that seemed to be daring me to smile back.

I was careful not to, since her first words to me, "Oh, another reporter," suggested she'd had her fill of outsiders who either smiled or laughed at SURAS. If so, I thought, she'd have to be more circumspect with her press releases.

"He's down from Indianapolis," McGregor told her, his tone making me think I might be the biggest catch to date. He added, "Like yourself, ma'am."

"I'm on a leave of absence from Eli Lilly," Dr. Tallion explained, naming the drug company that was Indy's prestige employer. Then she immediately shifted our focus. "You've picked an exciting day to visit. The magnetometer just detected something big. It could be a steamship's boiler."

"Is that right?" McGregor said and hurried off to see for himself.

"Hank's caught the bug," the director explained. "And he was a thorough skeptic when we showed up on his doorstep."

I said the SURAS theories must be compelling, giving her an opening she didn't immediately take.

"Addicting," she said instead as though warning me.

Word of the magnetometer reading must have been spreading through the gypsy camp. There was some scattered cheering and even a little impromptu dancing. Tallion considered the celebration with her fixed smile and then turned toward the river.

"We might have a quieter talk over there," she said and led me toward the levee.

As was often the case when the river was high, it was also brown, the shade nearly identical to that of the far bank.

"The Ohio's eating away at a lot of little McGregor farms today, all up and down the valley," Tallion observed from our vantage point. "Erasing the work of generations of farm families. It's waiting to wash away our work here. But it's evenhanded, the river. It buries suffering, too. It buries the dead.

"The *Utica* was a Union hospital ship, carrying home survivors of the Battle of Chickamauga. No one knows exactly why her boilers exploded, though there are theories: excess pressure, poor maintenance, Confederate sabotage. The explosion killed a great many—the *Utica* was carrying over seven hundred souls though her legal limit was half that number—but the real killers were the fire that took hold and the river.

"In addition to the soldiers, the steamboat carried a number of women, the wives and sweethearts of wounded men who had gone south to tend to them. One of reunited couples was named Rascoe, Lieutenant William Rascoe and his wife Lyla. After the explosion, they had to choose between the fire and the Ohio. They chose the river. For a time, they clung to a log. Like that one, perhaps."

She pointed to a tree trunk heading west at a good clip in the brown water.

"Then Lyla slipped away and was lost forever. Imagine the

powerful emotions Lieutenant Rascoe must have felt, what sorrow, what guilt."

The director paused to give me a chance to do my imagining. I thought she was dwelling on the lieutenant's understandable reaction as a way of heightening her story's effect. I was wrong.

"Then something strange happened. Rascoe looked up and saw a second steamboat coming around a bend in the river. Coming to their rescue, he hoped. It occurred to him that the ship looked very like the *Utica*, might even be her sister ship. An instant after he'd had that thought, the second steamboat exploded. Rascoe watched in horror as the passengers began to jump overboard, including a couple who leapt from the bow hand-in-hand, as he and Lyla had.

"The lieutenant came to shore on the Indiana side. He was taken in by a farm family, perhaps Hank McGregor's ancestors. When he recovered, Rascoe was shocked to learn that there had been no second steamboat disaster that night."

Again the director paused, this time for my explanation. I suggested that Rascoe had suffered a hallucination brought on by shock and hypothermia and guilt.

Tallion nodded a touch condescendingly. "There's another oddity connected with the *Utica* disaster. Upriver a little distance is the town of Jeffersonville. It had an army post in 1863. The officer on duty that night had been told to watch for the *Utica*. He saw her pass by safely about the time her wreckage was settling onto the river bottom. He telegraphed his report to Cincinnati."

There went his cushy posting, I thought. I said what I knew Tallion was waiting for me to say, which was that the Jeffersonville watch keeper had simply mistaken another steamboat for the *Utica*. Then, because I was tired of her smile and her knowing nods, I asked her how SURAS would explain those two sightings.

"We'd reference quantum physics, of course," she said. "Specifically Hugh Everett's theory of concurrent worlds. I won't bore you with the particulars; I'd confuse us both trying. My field is microbiology, not quantum mechanics. But Everett believed that the multiple outcomes possible from the behavior of certain subatomic particles may mean that multiple universes exist, one universe for each possible outcome. These infinite universes would contain every possible variation on reality as we know it and on history. There would be a universe in which Rome never burned and one in which Kennedy wasn't assassinated."

She watched the river for a time and then turned to face me, the crisp movement making the empty sleeves of her sweater dance.

"SURAS is dedicated to the proposition that multiple universes exist. It was founded just after the original *Utica* wreck was discovered in 1989. A Purdue University professor named Win Hadley happened to be a Civil War buff and knew about the sightings of alternate *Uticas*. Those sightings reminded him of Hugh Everett's theory of many worlds. Hadley wondered if Lieutenant Rascoe had seen an alternative universe in which the *Utica*, delayed for a few moments for some reason, exploded and burned in a different location. The officer in Jeffersonville might have glimpsed a reality in which the *Utica* didn't explode. Hadley founded SURAS to explore the *Utica* sightings in order to prove Everett right."

If SURAS dated from the late eighties, Tallion must have joined as an undergraduate. But I didn't ask her about that. She'd presented me with an opportunity to show off some arcane knowledge, and I couldn't resist it. As it happened, I knew a little about Hugh Everett's many worlds theory, including a corollary that made SURAS's efforts a waste of time. If I was remembering it right, Everett believed that his infinite worlds were non-communicating. Nothing, not a subatomic particle or a steamboat, could pass from one to another.

I trotted that out for Tallion. If anything, her smile became more serene.

"That's absolutely true, in the normal course of events. So if some exception to that rule occurs, if multiple *Uticas*, for example, are seen in a single reality, some powerful force must be at work, something capable of causing a momentary bleed-through from another reality, if not an actual breach. We believe that powerful force is human emotion, the concentrated pain and fear and loss felt by hundreds of souls at one instant in time."

If SURAS had one foot on the dock of science, it surely had the other in the New Age canoe. That probably explained its attraction for the Deadheads, aging and otherwise, who had begun to poke at McGregor's field with picks and shovels. Why the society would appeal to a microbiologist was another mystery entirely.

This microbiologist seemed to be waiting for objections, so I stated one, using as my example a different shipwreck, one that had always fascinated me. I said that if the SURAS theory was right, if human terror and pain could cause a "bleed-through" from one universe to another, the bottom of the North Atlantic should be littered with wrecks of the *Titanic*.

"Who's to say it isn't?" she countered. Then she showed off a little arcane knowledge of her own. "Did you know that some of *Titanic*'s passengers saw the ship break in two as it sank while others—the majority—swore that it hadn't? For seventy years, the official position was that the ship had gone down in one piece. But when they found the *Titanic* on the ocean floor, it was broken in two. Were more than half of the eyewitnesses wrong? Were they hallucinating? Or had they been granted a glimpse of another reality?"

Hank McGregor interrupted before I could reply. One look at his flushed face and I knew Tallion was correct about one thing at least. The farmer had definitely caught the SURAS bug.

"There's something down there all right," he said. "But you're not going to get much done with shovels. I've got a backhoe. I'll bring it down if you want."

Tallion, who'd been watching the efforts of the SURAS rank and file like an indulgent mother whose children had found a sandbox, accepted the offer. While they were discussing the details, I stepped away and took out my cell phone.

McGregor called after me. "You won't get a signal down here, mister. Sorry. But you're welcome to use the phone at the house."

He and I drove back together, and he showed me into a trim farmhouse that must have been furnished by his great grandmother and not changed much since. In the front parlor, we came across a napping woman whom I mistook for that long lost interior decorator or maybe her daughter. McGregor's first words to the white-haired woman told me she was actually another guest.

"Your people found something, Mrs. Hadley."

"Oh dear," the woman replied. "I guess I should go down."

The farmer led me to the kitchen phone and then hurried out. I returned to the woman in the parlor, who had yet to get out of her chair. I understood the delay, as she was squeezed into the chair so tightly she overhung its arms on both sides. I introduced myself and asked if she was related to Win Hadley, the founder of SURAS.

"I'm his widow," she said. "Winfred passed away in 2003."

I made what I thought was a polite remark, something about how proud the late founder would be of all the society had undertaken.

"Proud?" the widow repeated, in much the same way that Hank McGregor had earlier repeated "scientists." She added, "He'd be dumbfounded."

To keep the conversation going, I asked if her husband had taught quantum mechanics. She laughed.

"Not unless Byron or Shelley wrote an ode to it. Winfred taught romantic poetry. That made him a second-class citizen at Purdue, I'm afraid." She pointed to the university's logo on her sweatshirt. "We turn out more engineers than English teachers up there."

I asked her how Hadley had gotten interested in multiple realities.

"He was interested in almost anything that was odd and impractical, like his poetry. He played the zither—or played at playing it. He designed solar powered model airplanes. He was a Civil War reenactor, one of the first. The Civil War was a special passion of his. That's how he knew about the *Utica*."

Somewhere outside, a diesel engine roared to life. A moment later, McGregor bounced past the parlor window at the controls of a tractor. The machine carried a backhoe behind it like a jointed tail.

"Oh my," Mrs. Hadley said.

Winfred Hadley might not have been practical, but the society he'd founded certainly was. I repeated that thought to Mrs. Hadley, and it seemed to upset her.

"It wasn't supposed to be this way. SURAS was the most impractical thing Winfred ever came up with. He never intended to find a second *Utica*. He only wanted to discuss the implications of a second *Utica*. SURAS was an excuse for him and his buddies to sit around and drink beer and smoke their pipes and talk about what the world would be like if Hitler had never been born or if Jesus had been Irish. It was strictly an armchair society. There was very little research and no archeology. Winfred only put 'archeological' in the society's name as a joke and because he needed another vowel for the acronym. This silly field work is all that woman's doing."

I asked if she meant Dr. Tallion.

"Of course. She joined SURAS a couple of years ago. I kept the society going after Winfred died because I was sentimental and because I liked seeing our old friends. I don't know how Elizabeth heard of us. One night she just showed up at the restaurant where we met. She never entered into the spirit of the thing; she was always so serious. I never dreamt she'd stick with it, but she did. She did more than that. She ran for director—we elect one every year—and won. The next thing I knew, new members were pouring in, crowding out the old hands. And money was coming from somewhere for an expedition to find a second *Utica*.

"I couldn't believe it. Imagine thinking you could actually find that poor old unicorn. And now she's done it. She's won after all. I suppose I should go down and congratulate her. Is it much of a walk?"

I promised to drive her down if she could wait until I made a quick phone call.

The call I placed on the kitchen phone was to a former reporter named King who now handled public relations for Eli Lilly. After he'd asked after half the people at the *Star Republic*, I squeezed in my question about Elizabeth Tallion.

"Do I know her? I used to think I did. She worked in microbiology. Very sharp—until she jumped the rails."

I asked him what he meant.

"Is this for publication? You sure? Okay. Elizabeth lost a loved one on 9/11. Her life partner, I'd guess you'd say. The woman was in sales for IBM and happened to be visiting the World Trade Center that morning. Elizabeth never got over it. She was on a leave of absence for a long time. Now she's on one again. I've heard she's fallen in with a wacko group, a religious cult or some kind of flat Earth society."

Or a combination of both, I thought.

"I've heard she's pouring all her money into it," King added. "It's a really sad case."

He tried to pump me for the latest information on Tallion, but not so hard that I gave him any. Back in the parlor, Mrs. Hadley had managed to separate herself from her chair. I got her into my Chevy and eased us down the rutted lane that McGregor had taken at thirty in his pickup. Perhaps because I'd just spoken to a man who handled public relations, I was thinking about the press release that had brought me to Reynolds, where no press appeared to be wanted. I asked Mrs. Hadley if she had issued it.

"Yes," she admitted. "I did that behind Elizabeth's back. It was supposed to be a cold water treatment. I was hoping a little publicity would wake these people up to how they're acting. I thought if I could embarrass them, I could save them. Now I'm the one who feels embarrassed."

The backhoe was hard at work when we finally reached the field. The men and women of SURAS were gathered around the hole it had made, all except the director. She was standing in the bed of a nearby pickup truck, staring off toward the river.

I parked as close to the excavation as I could, for Mrs. Hadley's sake. As I helped her from her car, McGregor shut off his engine. He climbed down from the tractor and scrambled into the hole he'd dug, followed by a couple of the nimbler volunteers. By the time we reached the pit, McGregor was climbing out, and his SURAS fever had broken.

"It's not a steamboat boiler," he said. "It's an old steam-powered thresher. It must have gotten silted over in the 1903 flood."

A moan went up around the pit. The only two faces that hadn't fallen belonged to Mrs. Hadley, who looked relieved, and Dr. Tallion, who was as calm and poised as ever. Perhaps she was consoled by the possibility of an alternative universe in which she'd found her *Utica*. Or another in which a far more serious tragedy had never occurred.

"We'll find it yet," she promised her flock from her station above it. "We won't give up until we do." Her steady eyes sought me out in the crowd. "We'll never give up hope."

She nodded to me one last time, a nod so deep it was almost a bow. I returned the gesture and took my leave.

# GRANDMA NOSTRADAMUS

E.N. Boxleiter, my boss at the *Indianapolis Star Republic*, often gave me the impression he'd welcome the end of the world. It would let him catch up on his sleep, for one thing, and stop the letters-to-the-editor plague once and for all. But when Boxleiter was actually warned of the coming apocalypse and even handed its exact date, he reacted with his usual cynicism.

"The Last Trump is on for February 4," he told me one snowy January morning. "Check it out. I won't start worrying until you put in for vacation time."

Boxleiter gave me a woman's name, Rose Rennick, and an address on Thirty-fourth Street. That stretch of Thirty-fourth was very near the point where I-65 cuts through the west side of Indianapolis. It was so near it, I could hear the trucks on the interstate when I climbed out of my car in the driveway of the once modern house. The snow had made a fairyland of the blue-collar neighborhood, flocking every branch of every tree and bush. But it hadn't done much for the little ranch. With its nearly flat roof, pink brick, and aqua trim, the house looked like a tourist who had gotten lost on his way to Florida.

The front door was opened by a man with a shaved head and bare feet. In between those naked extremes, he wore sweat pants and a T-shirt advertising a local tavern.

"I'm Bud, the boyfriend," he said after I'd identified myself as a reporter. "I'm the one who talked Rose into calling your paper. Excuse the mess. We've got to pack everything up before we can turn this place into cash. It's been a pain, but without the packing, we never would have found the predictions."

He led me down a short hallway, past a kitchen whose floor was covered with stacks of canned goods and dislodged drawers of silverware and miscellaneous utensils. The passage ended at the living room. In the center of its shag carpet was a double row of boxes that held books, framed pictures, clocks, lamps, and assorted bric-a-brac. I decided that this collection was the previous contents of the room, which had been stripped of everything but a few large pieces of furniture. Beside the boxes sat Rose Rennick.

She was a slender young woman with the reddest hair I'd ever seen. It looked perfectly natural in combination with her pale, slightly freckled skin and her eyes, which were almost the same unlikely shade of blue as the tropical trim of the old house. She was dressed in scrubs, also blue.

Rose stood to shake my hand, and I noticed that she was holding a framed photograph. She held it slightly behind her, concealing it from me, I thought at first. But when Bud left in search of exhibits, she held the photo in plain view while she looked around the room. I saw then that it was a small group shot of Rose, a man who wasn't Bud, and a baby with red hair. Without a word to me, Rose slipped the picture between the cushions of a sofa.

Bud was reentering the room by then, carrying four books. "Did Rose tell you about this place? Go on, darlin'."

"It was my aunt's house," Rose said in a husky voice. "My Aunt Mildred's. Before that it belonged to my grandparents, Aunt Mildred's parents. She lived here and took care of them and then stayed on when they died. Now she's gone, too."

Rose paused to sniff, and Bud took over. "Rose's own folks are dead, so she's all the family that's left. That makes us the cleanup committee for this place. We've got an auction guy coming to haul everything out, but our lawyer told Rose to go through the house first, looking for keepsakes and valuables. What makes it such a job is old Mildred never threw out her folks' stuff, so it's like three people just died, even though the grandfather passed away in '86 and the grandmother in '95.

"Our lawyer said to be especially careful with the books,

'cause people hide money in books sometimes. That's how we found the predictions. They're all in the handwriting of Rose's grandmother, Iva Faye Clinger." He poked the introspective Rose. "Show him a picture of her, darlin'."

Rose went to a box marked "keep" and extracted a color photograph of a woman whose hair was a slightly faded shade of Rose's red and whose expression was soft-focused peace. Her granddaughter's expression was, at that moment, sad and strained.

"That's her," Bud said. "That's Grandma Nostradamus. Dead ten years this July. Sit down, and I'll show you what we found."

He pointed me to the sofa, and I sat down on the cushion to the left of the hidden photograph. Rose took the cushion to its right. Bud sat down on my free side, the books on his lap. He handed me one.

It was a cookbook called *Modern Recipes*, published by the Purdue University Extension Service in 1946. On its flyleaf was written "Iva Faye Clinger" in a clear though very circular hand.

"Flip through it," Bud said. "I left the paper exactly where I found it."

I did as I was told. Stuck between pages fifty-seven and fifty-eight was a slip of notepaper, yellowed with age. The paper was covered with Iva Faye's distinctive script. Most of what she'd set down was a recipe for something called "pie sauce." But at the very top of the slip, in a different color of ink, she'd written the word "microprocessor."

"What do you think of that?" Bud demanded as soon as I looked up. "On a piece of paper that's been in that book since maybe the forties, she wrote a word that wasn't even coined until 1970. I called the Central Library and they looked it up. How can you explain that?"

I told him that Iva Faye had probably used the pie sauce recipe sometime after 1970. While the recipe was out, she'd heard "microprocessor" on the radio or television and had written it down on the handiest slip of paper so she could research it later. It suggested curiosity to me, not second sight.

"Fair enough," Bud said. "I thought the same thing myself. Then I found this."

He handed me a book whose title was *Popular Hymns and Occasional Songs*. It had been published in Cincinnati in 1935. The inside cover was stamped with the name of an Indianapolis church.

I flipped through it and found an index card on which was written a list of song titles. Most were hymns I hadn't heard in years, "The Old Wooden Cross," for example, and "Shall We Gather at the River." At the top of the list was the word "Columbia," with a line drawn through it, a dramatic slash.

"That could be a prediction of the Space Shuttle *Columbia* explosion," Bud said. "Iva Faye died eight years before it happened, and that card could be even older. Maybe way older."

I opened to the index of the book and pointed to the title of an old patriotic anthem: "Columbia, the Gem of the Ocean." I suggested that Grandma Iva had planned to include the song in a church service or some other program and then had dropped it at the last minute.

"It could be both things," Bud said. "A song she decided to scratch and a prediction. I mean, she might not have known herself why she wrote that word down and crossed it out. Not the real reason, I mean. I don't think she knew she could predict the future."

"She didn't know," Rose said, sounding relieved about it. I thought of the photograph hidden between us.

Bud handed me another book. "This one's not as serious, but it's still pretty amazing."

The slim green volume certainly had a less serious title: *Sports Illustrated Baseball*. It had been published by J.B. Lippincott in 1958. The flyleaf bore the name and address sticker of William Clinger.

"My grandfather," Rose said. "He was a big fan."

The book might have belonged to Rose's grandfather, but the piece of paper stuck in the chapter on pitching bore the handwriting of her grandmother. The note read, "Socks (4)."

By this time, I was up to speed. I asked Bud if he thought the note referred to the Boston Red Sox's World Series victory of 2004.

"Right," he said. "The four could refer to the year or to the four games it took the Sox to do it."

Or to the number of bases plus home plate. I pointed out that Boston didn't spell its team name the way Iva Faye had and that the note was likely the beginning of an abandoned shopping or packing or laundry list. I didn't expect that to faze Bud, and it didn't.

"If you study the predictions of the real Nostradamus," he began a little pedantically, "you'll see that the spelling's off a lot. In fact, nothing's really black-and-white. You've got to look at things a little sideways to understand what he meant. And like I said before, Grandma Iva may not have known she was making a prediction when she wrote that down, any more than she knew she was naming the last day when she wrote this."

He patted the last book he held, which was bigger than the other three combined and covered in cracked, black leather. Bud didn't make me flip through this one. Instead, he opened it to a page very near the book's back cover and passed it over.

The tome was a Bible, as I'd guessed, and an old one, judging by its Gothic typeface. Bud had opened it to the last book of the New Testament, the Book of Revelation. Stuck between the two pages displayed was a triangle of browned newsprint. I would never have looked at it twice if I'd been paging through the volume. Not before meeting Bud and Rose. Now I turned the crumbling fragment over carefully.

On its hidden side was written "2-4-5" in a faded but familiar hand.

"We aren't Bible people," Bud said, "but I know that Revelation is called Apocalypse sometimes. It's all about the end of the world. So when I saw that date in Iva Faye's writing tucked in that particular spot, a date that's less than a month away, I knew we should tell somebody.

"I mean, it might not be the end of the world. It might be that some other big thing is gonna happen. But just in case, people might want to get themselves ready, get their knots untangled, you know."

The telephone rang. "That'll be the auction guy," Bud said and left us.

I waited until I heard him engaged in conversation in the kitchen. Then I pulled the hidden photograph from the space between the cushions.

Rose didn't object, but she did sniff again. Then she said, "Thanks for not saying anything. I didn't want Bud to see it. It's my baby girl and my husband, the ones I left for Bud."

She looked around the stripped room. "Aunt Mildred really got on me for doing that. Thank God Grandma Iva never knew." She added, less certainly, "I hope she never knew."

In the kitchen, Bud was wrapping up the call. I slipped the photograph back into its hiding place and stood up. Bud had no problem with the interview being over. Like many of the people I talked to, he was content to have had someone listen to his story.

But at the front door, he did make one last pitch for that story's publication. "Seriously, people should know about this so they can make up their own minds. And so they can spend the last day the way they want. In church or whatever."

He put his arm around the red-haired woman and squeezed her. "I know what Rose and I will be doing, but I'm not gonna tell you. Wouldn't want it to get in the paper."

Rose blushed dramatically, giving the secret away. I thanked the couple and left.

Back at the *Star Republic*, I told Boxleiter that I wasn't putting in for vacation time. I asked him if he wanted to hear the story, and he said no, barely looking up from the copy he was editing the old-fashioned way, with violent strokes of a red pencil.

February 4, 2005, Judgment Day, was clear and cold in Indianapolis. So cold that, if the world had ended by fire, as some people say it will, the first few minutes would have felt pretty good. But the world didn't end, by fire or any other way.

The next day, I drove back to the old house on Thirty-fourth Street. I wanted to talk to Rose and Bud again, though mostly to Rose. I was hoping that, it being Saturday, the couple might be there again, boxing up Rose's ancestors.

There was a car in the driveway, but it wasn't the black

Trans Am I'd seen on my prior visit. And the man who answered my knock wasn't Bud. I recognized him from the secret photograph as Rose's deserted husband. And the carrot-topped toddler who peeked out at me from behind his legs was surely the couple's daughter.

Rose herself—a smiling Rose—came next. She introduced me to her husband, Jim, and asked him for a moment alone with me. He carried the squirming child down to the basement to "practice our pool."

I wasn't sure why I'd come, unless it was to see how Bud and Rose were facing the morning after. I'd never know how Bud was doing, but Rose was radiant.

"We're going to keep the house," she told me. "Keep it in the family for another generation. Maybe two.

"I called Jim yesterday. I couldn't stand being away from him, not if the world was going to end. And he took me back. It's just like a miracle. I would've been content for the end to have come last night, with Jim and me and little Faye all together, but I'm happier it didn't. I'm happy that wasn't what Grandma's note meant."

I asked her what she thought the note did mean.

Rose's pale face blushed at about half its capacity. "I know you don't believe in the predictions, from your paper not running a story about them. But I can't help thinking that Grandma knew February 4, 2005 would be the most important day of my life, the day I went back to my family.

I think that's why she wrote two-four-five. In a way, she brought Jim and me back together."

I thought the unlucky Bud had actually had more to do with it, by discovering the "predictions" in the first place and by going on about people getting knots untangled before the end.

But I decided it was best to leave Bud out of it. I wished Rose luck with her new old life and her new old house and left.

On Monday morning, I happened to visit the cubicle of the *Star Republic* staffer who did the paper's religion page, a woman named Durbin. I told her the story of Iva Faye Clinger's predictions, which was still on my mind.

"That boyfriend was telling the truth when he said he and the granddaughter aren't Bible people," Durbin observed. "Anyone with a Bible-study background who found those numbers wouldn't think of a date. A Bible person would think it meant a chapter and a couple of verses. In Revelation, if that's where the note was found."

Durbin might have gone on to criticize my own religious training, but her phone rang. As she answered it, she pulled a Bible from a desktop rack and handed it to me, indicating with a wave of her thumb that she needed some privacy.

I carried the book to the nearest window. The cold from the frosted glass stole over me as I read the Book of Revelation, chapter two, verses four and five.

"But I have this against thee, that thou hast left thy first love. Remember therefore whence thou hast fallen, and repent and do thy former works."

# EMANATIONS, GREAT AND SMALL

Minerva Fine was a retired Indianapolis librarian who offered her services to the world as a mystic and medium. She was a genuine anachronism, a survivor from the days when séances were serious business in respectable Midwestern parlors. Her Aunt Ethel and Grandmother Flavia had both been mediums, but Minerva had specialized in a way that cut her off from family tradition. She only spoke with the spirits of animals.

When I first heard about Miss Fine from my favorite aunt, I reacted cynically. I knew that Americans spent billions of dollars a year on their pets, with my fellow Hoosiers chipping in more than their share. I was sure a doggie medium could only be after a piece of that bounty. But according to my aunt, who was a member in good standing, like Fine herself, of the Central Avenue Reformed Presbyterian Church, the medium never accepted payment for her services, which were almost exclusively performed for other ladies of the aforementioned congregation. Fine lived on her library pension and on a trust set up by her mother, a freethinker and one of the first female veterinarians in Indiana.

Nevertheless, I decided to expose Minerva Fine, young and self-righteous journalist that I was. That was how I pitched the story to E.N. Boxleiter, my editor at the *Indianapolis Star Republic*, as an exposé, a service to gullible church ladies everywhere. Boxleiter, after muttering something about cub reporters with too much time on their hands, wished me luck.

I called Fine for an appointment, and she agreed to see me the following day. Her address, like that of her church, was on Central Avenue, on the near north side of Indy. It turned out to be a large house, in some disrepair, surrounded by others in total disrepair. One of her front doors held a pane of beveled glass frosted in an elaborate design. The other door had a plain glass replacement backed by a white, lace curtain whose pattern came close to that of the beveled pane. Together they summed up the place for me, suggesting not so much dilapidation as an orderly retreat. Her doorbell was the old manual kind that looked like an equally ancient skate key. It turned easily and produced a grinding noise that must once have been a ring.

The medium answered the door herself. In appearance

she was pretty much what I'd expected: small and gray and dressed neatly in some distant fashion. Her eyes were exactly what I'd expected. I'd told myself that, if she were legitimate, she'd have open, vague eyes, probably in blue, the innocent eyes of an honest person who believed in something outlandish. Eyes that you looked into. Instead, she had another kind entirely, the kind of eyes that look out at you, revealing nothing from within. They were blue, as it happened, but it was a blue so dark it left the pupils ill-defined.

Fine took me into a small sitting room in which a card table had been set up. Two other ladies were already seated, Mrs. Dorothea Petty and Miss Jean Gerard, both Central Avenue Reformed Presbyterians. I asked Fine for some background, but it was Petty, a cheerful woman with suspiciously black hair, who responded.

"Animal spirits are much more difficult to work with than human ones," she began. "They never tell us what kind of animal they are because of course they don't think of themselves in those terms. They usually describe some experience they've had, and we figure out what species they must have been."

I asked for an example.

"Well," Petty explained, "the first time we contacted an animal spirit we were actually calling on our former pastor, Mr. Brust. He kept telling us odd things, for instance that he was sitting on the branch of a tree staring down at a black dog. We finally figured out that it wasn't Mr. Brust at all. We'd contacted Fluffy, a calico cat Mrs. Brust used to keep. Jean, here, was always a favorite of Fluffy's. Her presence made the link possible."

Gerard, a young woman with long slender hands, looked down at those hands modestly.

"We've found that that is the necessary ingredient for a successful contact," Petty continued, "a human participant who has some strong connection to the animal or the event described."

Petty went on to tell me about other contacts with cats, a few dogs, and a disconsolate love bird. All through the telling, Fine watched me, her royal blue eyes daring me to follow my initial impulse and laugh at the whole thing. I settled for interrupting Petty with a question. I asked her how the spirits of animals were able to speak at all. Fine answered this herself and impatiently.

"A spirit communicates in thoughts, not in words. It is the function of the medium to verbalize those thoughts. That's why there is no language barrier in psychic communication. Animals have thoughts to communicate, even if they are only very limited visual images. The more intelligent the animal, the more vivid and detailed the image."

Fine's tone suggested that I'd come in slightly less clearly than Fluffy. I tried to win her over by mentioning an English setter named Tag, a beloved childhood friend I'd never actually had. It wasn't an elaborate trap, but it was all I thought I needed. Fine then recited the standard disclaimer about bad attitudes causing bad séances while Petty lowered the yellowed shades.

Following their lead, I placed my hands on the table, palms flat and fingers extended. My little fingers touched Petty's hand on my left and Fine's on my right. Across from me, Gerard stared intently at the tabletop. I was about to ask how we would begin when I realized that this warm, dusty silence was the first step.

Fine closed her eyes. After a moment or two, Petty leaned forward slightly. I glanced back to Fine in time to see her pale lips move. They stopped, and Petty expressed her disappointment with a small sigh. We sat in silence for perhaps five minutes, during which time I saw traces of at least two other nibbles. Then Fine opened her small mouth and began to moan. It was a remarkable sound, coming from the petite, gray woman, almost an indecent sound. It was extremely deep, surely from the very bottom from her throat, and it rose and fell very slowly, each cycle taking ten or fifteen seconds. At the bottom of each swell, the sound gurgled.

"Oh my," Petty said. "It sounds like a big one."

I was beginning to enjoy myself when I noticed something strange. Fine's little finger had become as cold as ice. I looked across the table for corroboration. Sure enough, Gerard was staring down at the pale hand touching her own.

Petty came in with her part a little late, I thought, taken

aback perhaps by the gurgling moan. "Spirit, please speak to us. Tell us what is foremost in your mind. Tell us your thoughts and feelings."

I had the impression that there was more to this spiel, but Petty stopped speaking when Fine opened her eye. It was her left eye, and she opened it wider than I would have thought possible, considering how tightly shut her right eye remained. Fine turned her head slightly to the right and stared across the table. The effect startled Petty, understandably. I was still inclined toward nervous laughter, thinking that we had contacted the spirit of an extremely large parrot, but the temptation left me when Fine began to speak.

She spoke in a deep voice, one almost as low as the bottom of her moan. An unearthly voice is a medium's stock in trade, I knew, but I was still impressed by the voice and by the feeling it conveyed of some great hurt.

"I never found it," the voice began. "Never found it again." Then, after a moment or two, "I hear something. Something I've never heard before. I look for it, but it's too dark to see. I see the sound of it instead. It's coming down to me. The sound is louder than any I've heard, bigger than any I've heard. Now I can hear more than the shape and its movement toward me. I hear groans and cracks and pops.

"I see it. It's right on top of me. I move down and away and its passing rolls me over and over. It passes me and passes me and passes me. It's so big. It's the biggest thing I've ever seen. It's still moving past me. The sounds from inside it are almost as loud as its passing. Sharp, painful sounds. Awful sounds. The sound of death. No, many deaths.

"I move after it down into the darkness. It pulls me along behind it in the awful noise I see behind it. The noise is almost more than I can stand, but I can't pull away. We go down and down, darker and darker. I've never been this far from the light. I've never been this long from the air. I call to it, but it doesn't answer me.

"I can't stay with it any longer. I leave it and go up. I'm bursting as I go, but I don't think of the air. I think of the thing I've left alone in the darkness. The greatest thing I've ever seen.

"I see a change above me and I know I'm safe. I know that I will go back down and be with it again. I will be with it again."

The last words gurgled into the moan that had begun the contact. The moaning lasted so long and became so faint at the end I thought the connection had been broken. Then the voice whispered, "I never found it again."

Fine closed her eye. We sat in silence for a minute or two. Then Petty rose from her chair and circled around behind me, making her own animal sounds, soft clucking noises. She shook Fine gently, and both the medium's dark eyes opened immediately.

"Goodness, I'm tired," she said. "Did we make contact?"

"Yes, dear," Petty said, "but it was so noisy and jumbled I couldn't make heads or tails of it. Did you, Jean?"

Gerard shook her head.

"Would you like to try again, Minerva?"

Fine looked at me and smiled for the first time. The experience that had disappointed the other ladies seemed to have satisfied her in some profound way. Her smile was conspiratorial. She expected me to share her satisfaction and, to my surprise, I did.

"No," Fine said. "I think I've had enough for one afternoon." She extended her hand to me. "Thank you so much for coming."

The day beyond the beveled glass seemed too bright to me. I went back to my desk and wrote my story. At the end of the article, I revealed the secret of my own satisfaction with the séance, which was also my own contribution to it. I'd carried to the old Central Avenue house, filed in some recess of my mind, the shadow of a famous ship, which I'd studied on and off since the age of eleven. The ship was the RMS. *Titanic*, which sank in the cold North Atlantic on April 15, 1912.

I delivered my copy to Boxleiter in person. He began reading it with me still standing in his office. Two pages in, he stopped and looked up at me.

"If this ends up being about a whale and the *Titanic*," he said, "one of us is going to be looking for a new career."

My reaction told him he'd guessed correctly.

"How could you be taken in like that?" he demanded.

I started to protest that Minerva Fine couldn't possibly have known about my fascination with the lost ship. Boxleiter cut me off.

"I seem to recall another volunteer job of yours," he said, "a feature I let you do last year on the *Titanic*. And I presume you gave the lady your name when you called to set up an interview." He flipped back to the first page of the story. "She used to be what, a librarian? Did it ever occur to you that she might have done a little library research on a so-called reporter?"

I expected his next comment to contain a suggestion or two on my new career path. Instead, after considering me for longer than he had on the day he'd hired me, Boxleiter handed back the story.

"Let's try to remember," he said, "that we carry press cards, not tarot cards."

I considered going back to confront Minerva, but I decided in the end that I preferred to remain in the middle ground of possibility between the dream she'd created for me and the wreck of it left by an iceberg named Boxleiter. Though I'd set out to prove her a fraud, I found I didn't like to think of her that way.

And I did think of her from time to time. Usually, it was to wonder whether Minerva's strange avocation wasn't in some way a reaction to her mother, the freethinking veterinarian, and perhaps to growing up on a too strict diet of rational thought. They made an interesting pair, those two, the mother who tended to the bodies of dumb beasts and the daughter who heard their souls. In that telling, Minerva Fine wasn't a fraud. She was a rebel, someone who would always thumb her nose at the rational world, so-called reporters included.

That was the picture of her I decided to keep.

# TAPS

The year Leon Hammerle died, 2009, was a bad one for the veterans of World War II, who were passing away at the rate of a thousand a day. The huge number of veteran deaths meant that not all received the attention their service merited. Many made do with a flag on their coffins and, if their local papers provided the service, the tiny image of a flag next to their obituaries. Leon Hammerle, who had served in New Guinea and the Philippines, was luckier than that. He received a guard of honor, a three-volley salute, a grave in a national cemetery, and taps played over that grave by a real live bugler. But Hammerle had come close to missing out completely. He'd had one foot, metaphorically speaking, in an unmarked grave in potter's field until a call from an old comrade had rescued him.

I knew of Hammerle because the newspaper I worked for, the *Indianapolis Star Republic*, had run a story on the dead man's rescue from oblivion. Hammerle had died alone in a two-room apartment on Delaware Street in downtown Indianapolis. No one who'd shared the building with him had known very much about the eighty-five-year-old loner. No family had been located. The unclaimed body had gone to the Marion County morgue. Then a call had come in to the county coroner's office from a fellow veteran, Elza Royer of Kansas City, Kansas. Royer, who contacted Hammerle regularly, had become concerned when he couldn't reach him. A subsequent call, from the coroner to the Office of Veterans Affairs, had confirmed Hammerle's veteran status and set official wheels in motion.

A day or two after that story had run, I was called into the office of E. N. Boxleiter, my editor at the *Star Republic*, to hear it all over again. I knew as I listened that there would be something more. There was always something more from Boxleiter. Usually it was a question in need of an answer. This time, it was more of an ache.

"Hammerle's service is tomorrow," Boxleiter told me. "It doesn't seem right. There should be at least one family member there to see the old guy off."

I wondered if Boxleiter, an "old guy" himself and a veteran, might be thinking ahead to a different lonely gravesite. But I didn't ask him about that. I told him I'd be happy to drive up to Grant County, where the Marion National Cemetery was located, to attend the internment and to file a story. Boxleiter only grunted, so I knew I'd guessed wrong about my assignment. I next offered to track down a living relative of Leon Hammerle. That got a nod out of Boxleiter, and I was dismissed.

I started by calling the rental office of the apartment building where Hammerle had lived and died, the grandly named Monroe Building. I spoke with the building's manager, who told me his name was Spoon. I never learned if that was his last name or first name or nickname.

"Mr. Hammerle was the ideal tenant," Spoon said. "No late rent, no damage, no complaints. No bad smells even—not until the end."

I asked how long he'd known his ideal tenant.

"Ten years. I worked that out yesterday. So Leon would've been about seventy-five when he moved in here. He used to walk someplace local for his meals. The Canary Café, when it was around, or the Elbow Room or the Old Point Tavern. That was at first. The last few years he ate a lot of delivery stuff, to judge by his trash.

"You're probably going to ask me about family, but I can't help you there. I watched the police go through Leon's things. There was a picture of a woman and a child—a boy—near his bed, but no names on it, not even a photographer's. It was an old picture, too. *I Love Lucy* vintage. The only mail we found was bills and junk mail."

I asked Spoon if Hammerle had ever talked about his former job or his hometown.

"Not that I can call to mind. He was from out of town; I

remember that much. Seems like he came from up north in Indiana somewhere. Maybe northeast. I know he lived and died with the Ball State teams, so maybe he went to Ball State on the G.I. Bill.

"I talked to that service buddy of Leon's, the Kansas City guy, after Leon passed. I happen to be up in Leon's place cleaning up when the phone rang. I'm the one who told Royer to call the coroner, so I guess I helped out getting Leon his army grave. I'm glad about that. I hated to think of him or his ashes down in that morgue for God knows how long."

I asked Spoon if he still had Royer's phone number.

"Sorry. Never thought to ask him for one."

In answer to my last question, Spoon said he didn't plan to attend Hammerle's service. I thanked him for his information. I was grateful for a couple of items in particular. One was his mention of the bedside photo of the woman and child, which suggested that Hammerle had had a family at one time. The other was the interesting fact that Hammerle had rooted for Ball State University.

Unlike Indiana's two big universities, Purdue and Indiana, Ball State didn't have much casual statewide fan support. If you rooted for the Cardinals, you probably attended or had attended Ball State or your child did or had or else you lived fairly close to Ball State's Muncie campus. Or you had lived close. Muncie was north and east of Indianapolis, right about were Spoon thought Hammerle might once have lived. So

I called Ball State's alumni office, but they turned up no Hammerle, Leon or otherwise.

Next, I called directory assistance for Kansas City, Kansas, looking for a listing for Elza Royer. When that failed, I tried Kansas City, Missouri, and got the same result. I was disappointed but not surprised. Fewer and fewer people were maintaining landline phones, not even senior citizens. And if Royer was as senior as I suspected, he might even be in some kind of assisted living facility.

The *Star Republic* had once had a library and a librarian, who would handle research questions for computer-challenged reporters. More recently, we'd been left to our own devices—those devices being the humming terminals on each of our desks—and I'd come to depend on a young coworker named Eric Neuman, who could get an answer from a computer in less time than it took me to type the question.

I stopped by Neuman's desk, told him I was looking for a prior address and next of kin for a recluse named Hammerle, full name, age, and last known address cheerfully supplied. None of it made Neuman cheerful, especially the age.

"It's tough to trace someone so old they don't have much of an Internet presence, if any," he said. "Especially without a Social Security Number."

I suggested he try the voter registration lists and tax rolls for Delaware County, where Muncie was located. If that didn't work, I suggested trying the surrounding counties.

Neuman observed that that was six additional counties for a grand total of seven. I congratulated him on his knowledge of Indiana geography and headed for the parking lot.

Once in my Chevy, I drove to McCarty Street and the nondescript building that housed the Marion County morgue. It had probably been a warehouse or a factory in a former life. The only modern touches were a skim of stucco through which the original brick showed here and there, and a long concrete ramp that rose in a double switchback to a door of very smoky glass.

I gained an interview with the assistant coroner, Dr. Thelma Hodges, whose full face was scored outside each of her dark eyes by deep laugh lines. At least, I suspected they were laugh lines. Dr. Hodges neither laughed nor smiled during our brief interview. She didn't know me, but she was familiar with the *Star Republic*. Thanks to an exposé we'd run on unsanitary conditions at the morgue, she both knew the paper and wanted nothing to do with its current representative. When she heard I was there about Leon Hammerle, she unbent slightly, though that didn't keep her from opening with a grievance.

"There's no satisfying you people. If we don't cremate an unclaimed body the day after we get it, we're warehousing rotting corpses. But if we'd promptly disposed of Mr. Hammerle, you'd have been on us for cheating him out of his fancy funeral."

I conceded the point, which happened to be true, and

asked who in the coroner's office had spoken with Elza Royer. It turned out to have been Dr. Hodges herself.

"Nice guy, very sharp for his age mentally. But not doing great otherwise. When I suggested he come for the funeral—I thought those Honor Flight people, the ones who fly veterans to Washington, might bring Royer over from St. Louis—he said he couldn't on account of being bedridden. That's a shame, since we couldn't locate any of Hammerle's family."

When I asked about that family search, Dr. Hodges grew defensive all over again.

"It's not our fault that we couldn't find any next of kin. A lot of people come to a city to hide themselves in a crowd. It happens in New York and Chicago and it even happens here. If a man cuts himself off from his roots, the coroner's office can't be held responsible. We can't whistle up a family for him when he needs it."

By way of exonerating her office, I told her the *Star Republic* had failed to trace any of Hammerle's family, though I was secretly hoping that Neuman had succeeded by then. Remembering my promise to him, I asked Hodges if the police had discovered Hammerle's Social Security Number.

"It was about the only thing they did discover. Mr. Hammerle was living on Social Security, God knows how. He wasn't getting anything from the Veterans Administration, at least no papers he kept, or we would've known he was a veteran. I contacted Social Security, but they wanted a copy of a death certificate before they'd release any information. And who knows how long they'd have taken then. We decided to go ahead without it. If we'd waited to find a family, which might not even exist, you would've accused us of stacking up corpses again."

I nodded at the injustice of the world, and that nod got me Hammerle's Social Security Number. As I stood to leave, Dr. Hodges grew sentimental.

"I keep thinking of that poor Elza Royer. He's the one you should be writing about. He got so het up about Mr. Hammerle missing his army funeral, he cried right on the phone. I bet he's all alone, maybe in a VA hospital. You should be looking for *his* family."

I phoned Neuman once I was safely back in my car. He was no longer interested in the puzzle piece I'd found, due to a triumph of his own.

"I found an old address for a Leon Hammerle in Mount Pleasant, in southern Delaware County. He shows up there in 1955, along with a wife, Renée, and a son, Timothy. They're all three in the 1960 census, but in the 1970 and 1980 counts, Hammerle appears alone. By the 1990 census, he's gone, too."

So Hammerle had left Mount Pleasant sometime before 1990, at least ten years before he'd shown up on Delaware Street. There had to have been one intermediate stop at least. As for Hammerle's family, they'd either died or they'd left him sometime in the 1960s.

Neuman had given me one reason to hope: Leon

Hammerle had lived in a small town. It's been my experience that a small town's oral tradition is at least as good as a big city's archives. So I took the address Neuman had found and headed northeast for Mount Pleasant.

The town didn't live up to the first part of its name, being situated on a flat stretch of State Road 35 just south of the Prairie Creek Reservoir, about five miles southeast of greater Muncie. But I was willing to concede the accuracy of the pleasant claim solely on the basis of Mrs. Ivy Fenty. I met Mrs. Fenty after knocking on a couple of doors on Poe Street, where Leon Hammerle had been living as late as the 1980 census, without finding anyone who remembered him. Without finding anyone old enough to remember 1980, in fact. Not until the second twenty-something I encountered directed me to Fenty, calling her "the neighborhood's memory."

Fenty was at home, but barely at home. That is to say, the woman, bent and wattled and nearly blind, was holding on to her little bungalow on the strength of a live-in caretaker. The aide went off in search of lemonade, while Fenty apologized in advance for its being instant. She would have had a hard time squeezing real lemons, as her hands were frozen by arthritis. However, her smile and the bright eyes behind her big, square glasses convinced me that she was still adept at producing metaphorical lemonade from whatever lemons life tossed her way. I unintentionally dimmed that smile and darkened those eyes by asking after Leon Hammerle.

"Oh, I remember Leon. He stayed on in that house for ten or fifteen years after his wife, Renée, left him. So sad. Then one day he sold out. To a young accountant named Duett. That's with two T's."

I made a note of the second T before moving Fenty back a step by asking about Renée.

"She divorced Leon and took Timmy, their boy, and left. Remarried, I heard. Let's see, what was her second husband's name? She resettled in Anderson, I think."

"Resettled" made it sound like Renée had headed for California, perhaps by covered wagon. In reality, Anderson wasn't much farther away from where we sat than Muncie. It was certainly within the search area I'd given Newman, though if Renée had remarried, she would have slipped through any net cast for Hammerles.

I needed her second husband's name, but I wasn't worried. Not with Ivy Fenty on the trail. She'd already recalled one syllable of that name and had the other cornered.

"Redfield? No. Redfern? No. Redford? No. Redmond? Yes. It was Redmond. David Redmond."

I don't know which of us was happier about that feat of recall, but I know Fenty was smiling again when I left her.

I next made my final call of the day to directory assistance. The computerized operator who answered and the human one who eventually came on the line failed to find an

Anderson listing for David or Renée Redmond. But there was a listing for a Timothy Redmond, who might once have been Timmy Hammerle. The phone company didn't supply Timothy Redmond's address. Eric Neuman could have whistled it up while I waited, but I was feeling nostalgic. And I was very near Anderson. So I visited its library and borrowed something almost as anachronistic as a reporter who knocked on doors: a city directory.

When I knocked on Timothy Redmond's door, I didn't get an answer. It was four-thirty by then, not quite quitting time, if there was such a thing as quitting time in this brave new century. In the hope that Redmond was another anachronism, a nine-to-fiver, I decided to sit in my car for a while before I started canvassing the neighbors. While I sat, I wondered why Redmond hadn't contacted the paper in response to the story about his father. It couldn't have been because he hadn't recognized the name Hammerle. He must have been around ten, give or take a couple of years, when his parents divorced. So he knew all about his roots. I was hoping that Redmond was just a member of the growing group that didn't take a daily paper. Or that he subscribed to the Anderson paper, the *Herald Bulletin*, rather than the state edition of the *Star Republic*. There was a third alternative, one I didn't like, which was that he'd read the piece and then used it to wrap up his breakfast coffee grounds and eggshells.

Before I could decide on the likeliest answer, a little Japanese pickup truck pulled into Redmond's drive. The man who climbed out was thin and balding and dressed, like me, in a well-worn suit and tie. An anachronism, for sure. In manners as well as dress, I hoped, as I crossed the lawn to him, and that proved to be true. Though he clearly didn't want to talk to me after I'd mentioned Leon Hammerle—my request for an interview pursing his thin lips down to half their size—he asked me in. I turned down his offer of a beer, being full of lemonade. After he'd found a beer of his own, we went out onto the concrete slab behind the house. It held Redmond's gas grill, a glass-topped table, and two webbed chairs. Something—the barely furnished house or the barely landscaped yard—told me that two chairs were one more than Redmond usually needed.

I let him get well into his beer before I began the interview, observing as I waited his frayed shirt collar, the heavy five o'clock shadow that had done the fraying, and the slightly bloodshot eyes that were entirely devoid of Dr. Hodges's laugh lines. When he finally asked to see my credentials, I handed him a copy of that day's *Star Republic*, open to the article about his father's rescue from obscurity. Redmond barely glanced at it before tossing it onto the table, and I knew my worst fears about coffee grounds and egg shells were true.

I asked Redmond if he'd known that his father had been living down in Indianapolis.

"Last I heard, Hammerle had moved to a cabin up in Michigan. I didn't know he'd come back. Before you ask anything else, let's get one thing straight. David Redmond was my father, not Leon Hammerle, not in any real sense. Not any more than if he and my mom had had a one-night stand and then he'd disappeared, which I wish he had."

I asked him why.

"He was a mean drunk." Redmond looked down at the beer bottle in his hand and then set it on the table. "When he drank, he beat my mom and he beat me. It was the war that did that to him, my mom always said, so we had to make allowances. If he'd been crippled in the fighting, she would have stood by him, she always said. So if he was emotionally crippled, if he was this closed-in guy who could never tell you he loved you, who'd go weeks without saying much of anything and then yell his head off over nothing, she had to stand by him the same way. And she did, for years and years, until finally she'd had enough."

I asked if his mother was still in the area.

"Yes," he said. "In Maplewood Cemetery, she and my real dad both."

The folded edition of the *Star Republic* was still on the table between us. Redmond slid it my way. "I know you want a nice follow-up story, but I'm not going to help you out. Mom didn't get a big funeral, just a few old friends and me. She certainly didn't get an honor guard or a flag on her coffin. But she was a victim of World War II, a veteran of it, as sure as if she'd been in New Guinea herself.

"I'm a veteran of it, too, a war that was over years before

I was born. Years from now, your newspaper will run a big story on the last World War II veteran dying—and it won't be true. There'll still be thousands of us left, the stunted children of that damn war. And none of us will get a newspaper article written about us when we die. Leon Hammerle's gotten more attention already than he deserved. He's not getting me at his funeral."

That seemed to be that. I got up to go, fairly certain that my host would let me find my way unaided. But Redmond's out-of-date manners kicked in again, and he saw me to the front door.

On the way, I remembered what Dr. Hodges had said about the sad situation of Elza Royer, the St. Louis veteran who had rescued Leon Hammerle from potter's field. I asked Redmond if he knew the name.

"Uncle Elza, I used to call him. He was in my dad's outfit. He used to drive over sometimes to visit. Things were always bad after Uncle Elza left, so Mom finally asked him to stop coming."

When I told Redmond that Royer was ill and maybe alone, he only shrugged. The "greatest generation" was getting no love whatsoever from Timothy Redmond.

I reported my failure to Boxleiter, and he took me up on my earlier offer to serve as witness at Leon Hammerle's internment. I started out early the next morning, picking up I-69 at Indy's edge and heading northeast. The interstate took me past the places I visited the day before, Anderson and Mount Pleasant and, finally, Muncie, home of Hammerle's beloved Cardinals. After an hour, I got off at the unfortunately named town of Gas City and cut over to State Road 9, which took me north to Marion.

The Marion National Cemetery had started life as a home for aging veterans of the Civil War, many of whom ended up buried on the grounds. The home had then cared for and buried veterans of succeeding wars. So many, in fact, that the place had been designated a national cemetery in 1973.

The property had many large trees and far too many perfectly straight rows of identical white headstones. Its drive circled a monument to the Civil War—three bronze figures crouched warily around a bronze flag—and led me to the administration building, which looked like a country schoolhouse done on a federal budget. As I parked, I glanced around for a little Japanese pickup. A cynic like Boxleiter would have scoffed at that hope. Correctly, as it happened.

I was greeted on the front walk by the facility's administrator, William O'Neil, a tall, bespectacled man with a soldier's posture and a pendant's grammar.

"It will just be you and I this morning. And the guard of honor, of course. They're preparing now."

Not wanting to broach the subject of Timothy Redmond, I responded by saying it was a shame that the man responsible for the service, Elza Royer, hadn't been able to attend it.

O'Neil's stiff posture became noticeably stiffer. "There's

something odd about that. I don't know if I should discuss it, as you're a newspaperman."

I told him I was currently just a mourner. I could tell that O'Neil didn't need much persuading. He was clearly anxious to tell someone about his odd something, even a nosy reporter.

"Elza Royer is dead."

I was seeing the headline of the story, VETERAN DIES AFTER SAVING ONE LAST COMRADE, until O'Neil scattered the thirty-six-point type.

"He's been dead for five years. It's absolutely true. I decided to check with the Veterans Administration people in St. Louis to see if Mr. Royer was under their care. The coroner lady, Dr. Hodges, told me he'd claimed to be bedridden. I wanted to tell him that Mr. Hammerle was in good hands. I found out instead that Elza Royer had died in 2004. He's buried in the Jefferson Barracks National Cemetery. And it's positively the same man; he was in Mr. Hammerle's unit."

I saw a new headline, VET SAVES BUDDY FROM BEYOND THE GRAVE, but O'Neil put paid to that one as well.

"Dr. Hodges told me that the man who'd called her was very sincere, that he even cried on the phone. Did she tell you that?"

I said she had.

"And she said the man specifically claimed to be a World

War II veteran, though he told her he would never receive a military funeral himself."

Dr. Hodges hadn't told me that part, but it sounded familiar all the same.

I told O'Neil that the Royer call had come from another World War II vet, one who'd chosen to use Royer's name for reasons of his own. I didn't add that this particular veteran had yet to be born when the war ended.

Somewhere on the grounds, a carillon began to play, signaling the top of the hour. A man in a full dress uniform appeared at the corner of the building and nodded to O'Neil. He and I set out to bury Leon Hammerle.

# A PRAYER IN WOOD

A disaster doesn't happen every day to fill up a newspaper's empty columns, though some years it feels that way. But something does come along nearly every day that's almost as useful: the anniversary of a past disaster. The big ones, like the Pearl Harbor attack or the Kennedy assassination, rate a mention every year. Others, like the killer tornadoes that swept through the Midwest on an April day in 1973, have to wait for a round-numbered birthday.

I was still in school in 1973, but ten years later I was a reporter working for an Indianapolis daily, the *Star Republic*. When my editor, E.N. Boxleiter, called me in to talk about an anniversary article on the April storm, I thought I'd be heading south to Hanover, the worst hit spot in Indiana. I was nearly one hundred and eighty degrees of the compass off.

"The Ohio Valley took the worst beating," Boxleiter told

me. "But that system was so big people were losing roofs here and there as far north as Peru. One town lost its soul. I want to know how it's bearing up."

He passed me a thin manila file and went back to the reading I'd interrupted. I slipped away without pausing to ask why a story about souls, missing or otherwise, should fall to me. From the earliest days of our association, Boxleiter had singled me out for a certain kind of assignment, the kind that was concerned with more than names and dates and other solid facts.

Still, I started with the who, what, and where of the story, which I found in the folder he'd given me. It contained exactly two clippings, both from post-storm issues of the *Star Republic*. The first had run on the morning after and was very brief. It told me that a single tornado had touched down in a Tippecanoe County farming community called Gootee. No one had been hurt and only one building had been damaged, but that one, a church, had been totally destroyed.

The follow-up story, which had run two days later, identified the victim as the Gootee Church of the Risen Savior. It was accompanied by two photographs. The first showed the church as a white, frame building with a squat steeple whose pointed, four-sided roof was topped by a simple white cross. In the second photo, the church was a pile of scrap. The only structure taller than a man was an upright beam with a single arm that looked like an overbuilt scaffold. To the top of this, someone had tied a white cross, perhaps the same cross that had graced the steeple. It gave the wreckage the look of a battered ship with its colors nailed to the mast.

That defiant attitude was echoed by the only person quoted in the story, the pastor of Risen Savior, the Reverend Ellis Offett. "We're going to rebuild it," the pastor was quoted as saying. "You bet we are. Every stick, just as it was. We're not sure why God gave us this test, but we're going to pass it."

They'd had their work cut out for them, according to the brief history of the church that filled out the article. Not because the church had been large; it had actually been small, as crossroad churches tend to be. But it had been built by the area's original German farmers, men who'd known about hewing beams and fitting them together from their experience of building cabins and barns. This example of their handiwork, which dated from the Civil War period and had been nominated for inclusion on the National Historic Register, had contained no nails or ironwork of any kind in its supporting structure. Nor would its replacement, according to the man in charge.

"We're going to use the same methods they used in 1861," Reverend Offett had asserted. "It will help us reconnect to those immigrant pioneers. Come back and see us in a year. You'll be amazed."

I was exactly nine years late taking the pastor up on his

challenge. I found Gootee in the upper right-hand corner of Tippecanoe County, which was about an hour and a half north of Indianapolis. The drive from the interstate on State Road 25 was through flat farmland. Many of the fields had already been tilled, but the soil was still black with the runoff of winter.

Gootee had a grain silo, a bank, a café, and, a little way from that urban sprawl, a small white church. My first glance told me it was the exact duplicate of the church from the before photo of the follow-up article. My second glance said, "Hold on a minute."

For starters, the building wasn't a church. Not anymore. It was, according to the sign that hung from the heavy beams of the front porch, the Gootee Community Center. A free-standing sign near the gravel lot where I parked advertised not a fire-and-brimstone sermon but the run of a musical play called *Once Upon a Mattress*. The building's tall and narrow windows held plain glass in place of the colored panes that appeared as various shades of gray in the old newspaper photo.

I didn't spot the most significant change until I'd stepped into the road to take a picture of the former church. I noticed then that the cross—the old symbol of defiance and rebirth—was gone. The short steeple now ended in a copper finial, green with age.

The center's double doors were locked, but there was a button for an electric bell beside them. A little work with that produced a young woman dressed for painting in a gray track suit well daubed with reds and blues.

"The box office isn't open," she said. "Or are you here about the aerobics class?"

I showed her my press card and told her I was there to do an article about the ten-year anniversary of the tornado.

"Before I came to town," she said, dismissing the storm as ancient history. "I've lived here four years."

I asked her if the community center had still been a church when she'd arrived.

"Nope. Wasn't anything then, just closed up. If you want some information about the theater season, I can give you a flyer."

She went back inside to get it, and I followed her. The entryway may have been where the aerobics class was held. A stereo was set up in one corner, and one wall was mirrored. Through another set of double doors was the nave of the church. Beyond no more than a dozen rows of wooden pews, a woman I hadn't met was painting scenery meant to represent a medieval castle. My eye was drawn upward to the exposed rafters, massive wooden beams that might have been hand-hewn. I looked for the heads of bolts or metal reinforcing plates where the beams met one another and saw only wooden pegs, each as big around as my arm.

The floor creaked as the first woman rejoined me, flyer in hand. I asked her if she knew anyone who'd been involved in the rebuilding of the church after the storm.

"I bet Orrin was. Orrin Rembusch. He builds scenery for us. Real sweet old guy."

Back on the front steps, I asked for Rembusch's address. She pointed down the street to the town's café.

"If there's coffee on, Orrin will be there."

The coffee was on at Martha's Nook—judging from the cup I was eventually served, it had been on continuously for about a week—and Orrin Rembusch was there. He was a heavyset, bull-necked man with a craggy face that stood out among the pale April faces at Martha's due to its dark tan. The explanation for that tan was contained in the color snapshots spread out on the table Rembusch shared with two other men. The prints showed him on a fishing boat someplace sunny and warm.

When I told him my business, Rembusch pushed the vacation photos toward his companions, told them to "eat your hearts out," and led me to a quiet table in the corner.

"I've been thinking about that anniversary myself," he said. He had pepper-and-salt hair unfashionably oiled and gold-framed eyeglasses that seemed too delicate for him. "Scary how fast ten years goes by at my age. Of course, a lot's happened since that darn tornado."

I'd had the same feeling since arriving in Gootee, but I didn't lead off with the big changes. I asked first if Rembusch remembered the night of the storm.

"Yes, but not because of the weather. That thunder buster wasn't any worse than a hundred others I've lived through.

We didn't even bother going down into the cellar. My wife Rena and I were watching the news coverage of the damage along the Ohio River when the phone rang. It was Chuck Findley calling to say the church was gone.

"Old Ellis Offett was there when we arrived, stomping around in the rain, mud up to his beard, looking like something out of the Old Testament. Right then and there—before the rain had even stopped—he got us church elders to promise to rebuild the place. And not just rebuild it. He made us swear to duplicate it, as near as we could."

The waitress arrived with my coffee, and Rembusch inquired after her numerous children by name. When she'd gone, I asked him how big the challenge of rebuilding the church had been.

"Mighty big. Almighty big, you might say. We didn't have any plans, of course, just old photographs. But we also didn't have the know-how. We'd all of us done some repair work on the older barns around here—mine's a year older than the old church—but none of us had built anything like that from scratch. And it was from scratch, too. One of the funny things about that tornado was how hard it hit in the second or two it was on the ground. I mean, I'd heard all my life what a tornado can do, but seeing it was something else. All the old beams in the church were so busted up that we couldn't save more than a scrap or two, which wasn't enough."

He sipped his coffee, said, "Not nearly enough," and shook his head.

"Another thing we had against us was a manpower shortage. The membership had never been big and had gotten a little gray, with kids going away to college and staying away. Or plain dropping out. Some of the men around here who didn't belong to the church, like my fishing buddies Al and Jim over there, offered to help, but Ellis wouldn't have it. He said the original church had been built by true believers, that the marks you could see in the old beams from their tools were marks of the builders themselves, that they'd worked their own faith into the wood. A prayer in wood, he called it.

"Come to think of it, Ellis Offett was the biggest challenge we had. He saw the tornado as a judgment on us for falling away from the old-fashioned faith and the rebuilding project as a kind of penance. Everything had to be done by us. And it had to be done the old way, which meant the hard way. Took us the better part of two years. Darn near broke our collective back. Drove some people clean out of the church. But we got it done."

And yet within a few years, the Church of the Risen Savior had closed. I asked Rembusch if the defections during the rebuilding had doomed the church.

"I wish I could say that was what happened. It would sound a lot better. But no. Ellis had been right about one thing. We had been falling away from the old faith. We each of us knew it in our hearts. We just didn't know our friends in the pews around us felt the same way.

"I remember sitting in that church years before the storm and thinking it didn't really matter whether I believed or not, there in that place built by my great-grandparents and the great-grandparents of my friends and neighbors. It was enough for me to be in that building, to see their ax marks in the old wood. To feel that connection to them and to their belief.

"But when I sat in the new church, I didn't feel anything. And I wasn't the only one. We hadn't put our faith into that building after all. We didn't have it to put in. Building it without faith had been an empty ritual, like showing up very Sunday and going through the motions. After Rena passed away, I stopped making the effort. A lot of people had by then. Reverend Offett finally gave up and moved north. He was selling cars up in Michigan City, last I heard."

Rembusch nodded to some recent additions to the lunchtime crowd. I put money on the table for my coffee and said good-bye. Rembusch shook my hand, lingering over it a little.

"I found a line or two that about sums it up. In Shakespeare, not Scripture. Rena had always wanted to see that play *Hamlet*. Before she took sick, she dragged me down to the Purdue campus, where they were putting it on. One snatch of it really stuck with me. It was when the villain, a king, tried to pray and couldn't. And he said, 'My words fly up, my thoughts remain below. Words without thoughts never to heaven go.' Works the same way whether the prayer's in words or wood, I guess."

I drove back to Indy, wrote my story, and passed it to Boxleiter, who didn't seem surprised by its ending. I wondered if he'd known all along that the church had closed and had only sent me up there for another credit hour toward my graduate degree in cynicism. I wondered but didn't ask.

Fifteen years passed, during which I seldom thought of the town of Gootee. Then one day I found myself in the neighborhood, so to speak. I was up at Lake Shafer, looking into reports of a giant snake, which turned out to be a prank concocted by two former employees of a local amusement park. On my way back, I decided to drive through Gootee to see how it was doing, twenty-five years after its soul had been destroyed.

The surprising answer was quite well indeed. I found the town surrounded by housing additions on which the paint was still drying. The business district now had a second bank and competing drug stores as well, and a billboard-sized sign identified the future location of a Walmart.

Most surprising of all, the Gootee Community Center had reverted to its original calling. It was now the Gootee Church of the Divine Light. Or a small part of it. Behind the old frame building, which had regained its stained-glass windows, was a structure the size and shape of an aircraft hangar.

All was explained to me by the pastor of Divine Light, Dr. Devon Newgate. Dr. Newgate was a young man with the ghost of a Jamaican accent and long thin hands that were never still.

"It's the automobile business that brought the town back," he said as he showed off the sanctuary of the new church, an auditorium that would have done a small college proud. "We have two different factories that supply parts for the big Japanese car plant down in Lafayette. New people moving in every day, a lot of them looking for Christian fellowship, which is what we offer.

"We started in the old church, believe it or not. It was closed up when I came to town and needed a thorough cleaning, but you could see it was a beautiful old place even then. The work on it began twenty-five years ago this year. It's a replica of an even older church, but you must know that since you say you've written about the tornado.

"We outgrew the old church pretty fast, but it's still an important part of our ministry. We use it for smaller weddings and as a meeting space for our committees. And I stop in almost every day to sit and pray. I love the new church, especially when it's full of people and song, but I always feel closer to God in the old church. I look up at those beams and I think of the folks who shaped them with such care and love. The marks in the beams are like handprints in cement, the prints of the old believers. I feel their faith, and it refreshes mine."

As he walked me to my car, Dr. Newgate pitched the idea of another anniversary article on the tornado, one that would feature his congregation. It would have been a well-deserved thumb in a certain editor's eye, but I knew I'd never tell Boxleiter about the reborn church. I was afraid he'd send them a copy of the article I'd done on the tenth anniversary, with key passages about lost faith and earthbound prayers underlined in red.

When we reached the parking lot, my guide pointed up to the old steeple, and I saw that a white cross once again stood at its peak.

"We're really proud of that. That's the original cross from the 1861 church. It survived the tornado somehow. When the replacement church was deconsecrated in the eighties, a local farmer stuck that cross away in his barn. Nice old guy named Rembusch. Orrin Rembusch. Dead now. He stored it for years like he knew we'd need it someday. Do you believe that?"

I told him I did, and we parted.

# BACK HOME AGAIN

Early one Sunday morning, a fisherman named Rudy Possman saw three men dumping something suspicious into Geist Reservoir, a large, man-made lake northeast of the city of Indianapolis. When Possman reported the incident to the police, they reacted as though he'd claimed to have sighted a Russian submarine. Many fishermen take pride in a reputation for tall tales, but not Rudy Possman. He called the *Star Republic* seeking vindication. My editor, E.N. Boxleiter, trusted me with the assignment.

I interviewed Possman at his favorite fishing spot, a causeway that carries Fall Creek Road across the reservoir's narrow waist. The road disappeared into a pine forest on our left. To our right, an artificial forest of aluminum masts marked the location of the Indianapolis Sailing Club. Beyond the bridge, through a white blue morning haze, I could see small wooded islands and the outlines of homes on the shore beyond.

Possman slapped the rusted metal railing that lined the causeway. "This is the spot," he said. "Any Sunday morning, you can find me right here."

Possman was an older gentleman with weathered skin, a stumpy beard, and slick hair more gray than brown. The broken brim of his baseball cap formed a tent-like peak that cast his pale blue eyes in shadow. The eyes were suspicious, watching me closely for a sign of disbelief. He rubbed his nose with the back of his hand and paused for a moment before continuing.

"It was about six a.m., just light. There was a cool breeze coming off the water, and it was hazy, hazier than today. I heard 'em before I saw 'em. I didn't hear the boat. They must've been out there before I set up. What I heard first was somebody asking, 'Is this the spot?' It wasn't said loud, but the water carries sounds right to you if the wind is right. Anyway, there was no answer, and I didn't think much about it. Somebody else fishing, I thought. Then, about five minutes later, the crying started. It sounded like a man crying. It wasn't too loud, but it was steady, and it kind of gave me the creeps coming out of the haze like that.

"The sun had come up, like I said, and it started to burn the haze off. That's when I saw the boat." Possman turned and pointed toward the center of the lake. "Out there about two hundred yards. There were three men in the boat, just sitting in it, not fishing or anything. The crying had stopped by then.

"They just stayed put out there for about twenty minutes. The cool breeze and the haze were gone, and it was already getting hot. I'd started to forget about 'em when I heard 'em trying to start their boat. It took 'em forever. I think they flooded it. When they did get it going they just wandered around out there, never much above idle and never getting anywhere. One of 'em was standing up all the time like George Washington. That went on for five minutes, maybe less. Then they stopped the boat and all three stood up. Two of 'em lifted something onto the side of the boat. I could tell it was something heavy 'cause it leaned the boat way over when they set it down. It was box- shaped, three, maybe four feet long and half as wide. They held it on the side of the boat for a second and then let it go over. It went down like a hunk of rock."

Possman looked toward the lake for a time. The weekday morning traffic consisted of a single boat running at speed and leaving a large wake.

"Damn inboards," Possman said. "They really cut the water up." He turned to face me. "I called the sheriff's office that same morning. I thought it was my duty to report it. Who knows what those bozos were dumping in there? Maybe it was the pieces of somebody they'd bumped off. There's a lot of killing these days in the drug business."

And the television business, I thought. I asked Possman what the sheriff's people had done.

"Nothing," Possman said. "Some deputy came and damn near wore himself out scribbling it all down. He said he'd be in touch with me. After two or three days when I didn't hear from 'em, I called again. This time, I talked to a deputy named Carlson. The bozo asks me if maybe I wasn't drunk that morning. Six a.m. on a Sunday morning!"

Possman's indignation gave way to a smile that was almost a wink. "As a matter of fact, I'd had a beer or so, but I don't start seeing things on two beers or even a dozen.

"Carlson ended up by telling me to forget the whole thing and not to bother 'em again." Possman banged his hand against the metal railing, this time as an expression of disgust. "I know what I saw," he said. "I don't know what they dumped, but they weren't throwing back blue gill."

Possman couldn't remember much about the boat. It was a small outboard, a fishing boat, maybe green, maybe brown.

I left Possman and took Fall Creek Road back toward town, looking for a pay phone. I found one outside a small marina. I called the sheriff's office and asked for Deputy Carlson. His name was one of the few concrete details Possman had given me. The deputy came on the line quickly. He interrupted my introduction as soon as I mentioned Possman's name.

"You're wasting your time," he said. "That's Geist you're talking about, not the East River. Nobody's dumping bodies in there, and if they did, they wouldn't fold them in half and box them up first. The guy was drunk. Give him a Bud, and he'll tell you about the great white shark he hooked the week before."

I asked Carlson if there had been any attempt to trace the men.

"No," Carlson said. "We'd have to search every beer can in town."

I thanked him and hung up. An electric bell rang loudly as I entered the marina office. The desk was staffed by a young man with spiked hair, who was wearing a short-sleeved, pink shirt and a narrow tie. He looked as though he would have been happier selling shoes in a mall somewhere. I asked him how many marinas there were on Geist.

"One that's open to the public," he said. "This is it."

I asked if they rented boats.

"Fishing boats," he said, "not speed boats. Ten horse, tops."

When I asked him if three men had rented a boat early the previous Sunday, the young man smiled. "What's the story on those guys? Some sheriff's deputy was in here Monday asking about them."

So much for Carlson's disinterest. I showed the clerk my press card and repeated the question. He pulled at his tie as he answered.

"The cop didn't tell me I should keep my mouth shut, so I guess it's okay. We did rent a boat to three guys on Sunday.

First thing. I thought there was something funny about them at the time. They were carrying fishing tackle, but one of them was dressed like he was going to church. No kidding, black wingtip shoes and all."

The clerk paused and his smile broadened. "Are you going to ask me about the box? The cop asked me if they were carrying a box, three or four feet long. I told him no, I didn't see one, but they could have carried anything from their car to the boat. I didn't watch them load. The funniest thing was, they didn't stay out very long. Maybe an hour, tops."

I asked the clerk if he'd gotten a name or an address from the men.

"Sure," he said. "You've got to show a driver's license to rent a boat." He turned over one page of the dog-eared ledger that lay open on the desk. "The cop didn't tell me to keep this quiet, so I guess it's okay. I'll write it down for you, if you want. I'll put my name here on the top, in case you want it later on."

The address took me to Lawrence, a community on the east side of Indianapolis, and to a street of modest, vinyl-sided homes. The house I wanted was distinguished from its neighbors by the light blue Lawrence police car that was parked at its curb. A uniformed patrolman answered the front door. I asked for Robert Vansickle, the name the marina clerk had given me.

"I'm Robert Vansickle," the patrolman said.

I introduced myself and told Vansickle I was trying to

trace three men who had been seen dumping something in Geist Reservoir on Sunday. He took a step backward and shut the door, hard.

I was halfway to my car when the door opened again. Vansickle called to me from the porch: "Come in here a minute."

He led me into the living room and pointed to a swaybacked sofa. I glanced around as I sat down. It was a sad looking room, worn out but not lived-in, like a waiting room in a hospital or a bus station. No family pictures. No personal clutter.

Vansickle placed himself directly in front of me, close enough to discourage me from standing. He wasn't a tall man, but he was big through the chest and shoulders. I guessed him to be about forty. His reddish brown hair was close cut and carefully combed. His pink face, which was showing early signs of jowls, was not improved by the expression it wore, which was unfriendly. "Now," he said, "what's your problem?"

I started to ask him if he'd rented a boat at Geist on Sunday, but he fired off his own question before I'd finished. "Just what makes this your business?"

I didn't enjoy being on the receiving end of the interview. I took a gamble and told Vansickle that he could talk to me or read about himself on the front page of the *Star Republic*.

There was a break in the dialogue. Vansickle stared down at me, and I stared up at him, both of us trying hard not to blink. At least, I was trying hard. Not blinking might have come naturally to him. Finally he said, "Wait here."

I heard him punch a number into a phone in the next room and say, "Earl? Get Billy and come over here quick."

He came back into the living room and leaned against the wall opposite the sofa with his arms folded across his chest. "It'll be a minute," he said.

Ten long minutes passed while Vansickle watched me and I discreetly studied the exits. Then I heard footsteps on the concrete walk. The two men opened the front door without knocking. They looked from Vansickle to me and then crossed the room to stand by the patrolman. They were each about his height, but thinner. They had the same vaguely reddish hair.

"My brothers," Vansickle said, "Earl and Bill."

He nodded toward each in turn. Earl, the thinnest and best groomed, was wearing a three-piece suit and a tie. I guessed him to be the fisherman with the black wingtips. Bill wore dirty work clothes, and his hands were dark with grease. His face was marked by random streaks of it that looked like charcoal slashes made by an angry artist.

To his brothers, Vansickle said, "This guy's a reporter from the paper. He wants to know about the business Sunday. My first idea was to send him walking, but then I thought no, he'd just keep poking around. We may have to tell him about it and take our chances. You guys gotta say."

Earl took a step forward. "What do you know?" he asked me.

I related Possman's story and the little I'd learned from the marina clerk.

When I'd finished, Earl said, "We don't want any newspaper story about this. What we want is privacy. We didn't do anything wrong, at least nothing we think is wrong. Can you keep quiet about this? I mean, if we tell you?"

I said that depended on what they'd dumped in the lake.

"It was our mother," Bill said. "Mary Holzer Vansickle."

What he'd said didn't make enough sense to shock me. I was more surprised to find that he had tears rolling down his cheeks. Robert put his arm around his brother's shoulders.

"That's it," Earl said. "That's what we did Sunday. We buried our mother out in Geist Reservoir. That was her last request, sort of."

Earl crossed the room and sat down next to me on the sofa, smiling as confidently as an insurance salesman calling on relatives. He took out his wallet and showed me a small photograph. It was a portrait of a square-jawed, unsmiling woman.

"Do you know how they made Geist?" Earl asked me. "It was back in the forties. The land was mostly small farms then, and one town, Germantown, just a crossroads and a country store. The state came in and condemned the land. Eminent domain. They bought all the farms and the town and told everybody to get out. We lived on one of those farms. It had belonged to my mother's family, the Holzers. At the time the farm was condemned, it was just Mom and the three of us living there. Her folks were dead, and Dad was buried with a lot of other soldiers over in France.

"Anyway, we lost the farm and moved here to Lawrence. Mom never talked about the old place much over the years. Not until about six months ago. She hadn't been so good for a while and she decided that she was going to die. She also made up her mind that she wanted to be buried on the old farm where she'd grown up and where her folks were buried. She didn't want to be alone."

I asked Earl if he was sure his grandparents were still under the lake. I told him that state law required the relocation of any bodies buried on condemned land.

Earl smiled patiently. "The state people wanted Grandpa and Grandma moved, but Mom wouldn't hear of it. It was their land, and she couldn't see taking them out of it. So she had the graves covered over, headstones and all. They're still down there all right. And Mom's with them.

"We worked it all out after she died. Turned out she was right about dying. If she'd made it another four months, she would have turned ninety, but she didn't care enough about that to try."

Earl leaned toward me and lowered his voice. "They wouldn't release the body to us, so we had her cremated. We had a regular service before that, with a minister and everything. We put the ashes in a box Billy made. It was sheet steel, weighted with lead. Sort of a monument and a casket both. That box will last a long time.

"You know the rest. We had some trouble finding the spot, even though we'd worked it out from some old maps. The farm was seventy acres though, so I guess we hit it."

Bill was crying steadily now, his eyes squeezed shut. I got up, embarrassed.

"The sheriff's people promised me they'd sit on this," Robert said. "Can we count on you, buddy?"

I told him they could.

On the way back to the office I put together a hard-luck story to use on my boss. Somebody had beaten me to it.

"I want you to put that Geist business on hold," Boxleiter said as I entered his office. "We don't want a scare about the city's water supply. I'll let you know what develops."

I thought I knew what would develop—nothing—but I was wrong. About four months later I got a call from Rudy Possman, the sensitive fisherman. He'd seen the same three men in the same boat on the same spot. I asked him if they'd dumped anything.

"Yes," he said. "Flowers."

# INTO LEGEND

________

October is the month for ghost stories. The cold, clear nights and early frosts suggest them. People on hay rides or sitting around bonfires scare each other with them. Respectable newspapers run them opposite recipes for pumpkin pie with accompanying staff illustrations of jack o' lanterns printed in two colors of ink. My editor at the *Star Republic*, E.N. Boxleiter, must have had a recipe that needed company. One evening in late October he sent me out to Avon, a small town just west of Indianapolis, to do a feature on its haunted bridge.

There's probably one haunted railroad bridge per county in Indiana. The tradition may be a holdover from the last century, when a roaring steam engine in the night was the most frightening thing most Hoosiers ever encountered. Avon's bridge is notable for its convenience, being only a twenty-minute drive from Indy, and for an especially gruesome detail of its legend: One of its ghosts is a baby.

My interview was supposed to be with the local sheriff, but some more important business had taken him away. In his place, he'd detailed a deputy who had gone off duty a few minutes before I arrived. Deputy Richard Sheffler was a tall man who looked like he'd once played football and could again if he wanted to. This impression was contradicted by his expression and by the gray in his hair, both of which made him look too serious for games. I decided that the curt greeting he gave me as we shook hands was my thanks for dragging him back out into the cold night after his shift.

We drove in silence for a mile or two back down the new four-lane highway toward the lights of Indianapolis. Then we turned right onto an undistinguished country road.

Immediately, the glow of the distant city and the lights of the highway were lost, blocked by the forest through which the road was cut. The road was narrow and winding and already lined with fallen leaves that were bright yellow in our headlights. The road split without warning and we took the left fork.

"That other's the road to Cartersburg," Sheffler said. "We call it the high road. It crosses the tracks just by the bridge. This is the low road. It goes under the bridge up ahead here and on to Plainfield."

Still descending, we rounded one last curve. Waiting beyond in the darkness was the bridge. Sheffler slowed almost to a stop and swung the cruiser's spotlight. In its moving beam, the bridge looked massive. The weathered brown arch that crossed the narrow gully through which the low road ran looked like it had been carved from the bedrock of the adjoining hills, but its pitted surface showed that it was really cast concrete. Above the arch, a low black wall of old iron hid the tracks from view. At one time, the ironwork had probably held the name of the railroad that owned the line. Now, all it displayed was an illegible tangle of multicolored graffiti. Sheffler held the light on the center of the arch. There the cement had been shaped into the outline of a keystone. It bore the year 1910.

I was startled by the sound of an unmuffled engine coming to life. Headlights came on in the trees to our left, and an old pickup appeared, waddling slowly through invisible ruts. Beyond the bridge, a second set of headlights snapped on.

Sheffler grunted to himself. "Another romantic evening spoiled. This is a major parking spot for the kids. Has been forever."

He waited until the retreating taillights had disappeared toward Plainfield. Then he backed the cruiser into the rutted lane from which the pickup truck had come. He switched off the lights and then killed the throbbing engine. There was no sound to take its place.

"That's the big haunted bridge," Sheffler said. "Worth the drive out?"

I couldn't see his face, but his tone told me that the

annoyed expression I'd seen earlier at the station hadn't faded away. When I asked him if he knew the story of the haunting, he grunted.

"Yeah," he said, "it's a real charmer. It's supposed to have happened fifty or sixty years ago. A woman was walking on the tracks one night, taking a shortcut from one farm to another. She was carrying a baby. She'd been to visit her folks or something. Anyway, she got to the bridge here and slipped and fell. Banged her head on one of the rails and was knocked out cold. Not the baby, though. It lay on the tracks crying out until a freight came through at high speed. Nice story, huh?"

He'd half turned in his seat and fired the question at me like a challenge. I felt the handle of the door behind me pressing into my back.

"Here's the best part," Sheffler continued. "When a train crosses the bridge, the iron roadbed that carries the track across the cement arch makes a noise like the world ending. Part of the noise is a high-pitched squealing that's supposed to be the sound of the baby.

"That's it, the haunted bridge legend. Just an old story some kids made up to scare each other with before they had slasher movies to go to. Stupid."

He emphasized this judgment by banging the steering wheel with his fist. For no reason I could see, he'd gone from irritated to plain mad as he'd told me the story.

"So what do we do now?" he asked. "Sit here till a train comes by? They're not as regular as they used to be."

I thought about it and decided that I was more interested in Sheffler's attitude than I was in the story of the bridge. I asked what was bothering him, and he looked startled for a moment, as though he was surprised I'd noticed.

"Sorry," he said. "I didn't mean to be rude. I know you're just doing your job. I'd be happy to help you out, most times. It's just that I hate this place. I hate the stupid story about it and everybody making it a big joke. It isn't a joke to me. A good friend of mine and his girl were killed here when I was in school. I saw it happen, and it still bothers me."

It sounded like he was going to leave it at that, so I asked him to tell me about it, off the record.

He shrugged. "Not that much to tell. If I really knew what happened, it wouldn't bother me so much. Why it happened, I mean."

He rolled his window down an inch and pulled a pack of cigarettes from his jacket. "Bother you?" he asked, holding one up. "Bad habit." He lit the cigarette with an old, steel lighter and blew smoke sideways out his window.

"Bill Whitmore was the kid's name. William Charles Whitmore. We grew up together in Danville just west of here. I called him Billy until we were about fourteen. Then he told me he was too old for that. From then on it was Bill. He was a nice guy, no rocket scientist and poor as dirt, but real steady. We played football together at Danville. We had this plan that we'd get into college on football scholarships and stay out of the army. This was back in '66, '67."

Sheffler turned away from me and settled in his seat, addressing his story to the steering wheel. "Something happened to Bill the summer before our senior year that changed him. That part was no mystery. It was the girl he was going out with, Marcia Terrell. I don't know how they ever got together. They were total opposites. He was quiet, and she was loud and flashy. She was fast, too, as we used to say back then, meaning she'd been around. Bill was nuts about her, couldn't think of anything else. He almost quit football, he was that gone. She must have wanted him to play, though, because he went out for the team senior year like always.

"So I know that part." Sheffler tapped the steering wheel with his fist, as though he were mentally filing that piece of the story away. "And I know the next part, which was that later that year, in the fall, Bill decided that he had to break it off with her. He said she was running his life, making big plans, smothering him, and that he was going to put a stop to it. There might have been more to it. He might have found out that she was going out on him. I never asked."

The burning tip of Sheffler's cigarette made a small orange arc in the darkness as he tapped the steering wheel again. "Now comes the part that doesn't make sense. They didn't break up. Something happened between them. I don't know what, nobody does. But the night of the wreck they were still together, and Bill wasn't right. He was kind of crazy, I mean, and distracted. We played Beech Grove that night, and it was no game at all. We could have beaten them with our cheerleaders. Everybody was kind of laying back except Bill. He was pounding those guys, hurting them, which wasn't the way he played.

"After the game, we drove into Indy to the Pole to eat like we always did, and Bill was like he was in a trance. He'd been drinking, too. Just a couple of beers probably, but that was big drinking in those days. Marcia was wired somehow. She couldn't stop talking. I mean, she always ran everything, but that night it was like she owned everything. I'll never forget the sight of those two sitting side by side. Mostly I remember their eyes, Marcia's darting around everywhere like searchlights and Bill's just staring off into space but glowing too somehow as bright as hers."

Sheffler took a long drag on his cigarette and turned his head to blow the smoke outside the car. "After we ate, the gang split up. The guys who didn't have dates went cruising, down to the Tee Pee, over to Frisch's, and back to the Pole. Big time stuff. The guys with dates had other plans, like ending up back at this bridge. That's what I did with my girl, Patti."

That name from the past snagged him for a few seconds. Then he shrugged and went on.

"We were here when it happened. We heard the freight train coming from a long way off. It was this kind of night, frosty and clear, and we heard the train first like a noise of wind in the trees. The drumming of the diesel got stronger. Then the engineer blew his horn for the Gale crossing, and it was loud and still miles away. That always got me going, because I knew he'd blow the horn again right above us for the high road crossing. I'd sit and wait for that, feeling the vibration start to come up through the car and watching the headlight of the big diesel starting to flicker on the ironwork of the bridge."

I looked up through the trees as Sheffler spoke and located the darker mass in the general darkness. Seen through the moving branches, the old bridge seemed to be swaying gently.

"Patti saw the car before I did. I saw her eyes get real big and her mouth open. I turned in time to see the headlights going past through the trees up on the high road, and then the car was there, going a hundred. I tried to yell, but I didn't have time. The train was already in the crossing, a heavy freight, two engines going full bore. The bridge was screaming, and the horn was blowing and rattling the car windows, so maybe I did yell and not hear it. The car hit the second engine without slowing down. The train carried it into the retaining wall on the bridge, and it fell onto the low road in a ball of fire.

"I was out of my car by then, but I couldn't get near the wreck for the fire. I suddenly knew it was Bill's Falcon—not from the way it looked in the road, it was just a shapeless pile—I'd recognized it without realizing it in the second when its headlights lit the side of the train."

I looked down from the bridge and found that Sheffler was facing me again.

"They said later that Bill must have been drunk and trying to beat the train through the crossing, but I never have believed it. The train was there way ahead of the car, and Bill never slowed down. Racing a train isn't anything Bill would do anyway, drunk or sober. They buried them and forgot about them, but I never have. I've never been able to stop wondering about that night, wondering about what really happened, I mean. I guess I won't know until I can ask Bill himself.

"Anyway, that's why I hate this place and the old, silly story about it. It's like playing in a cemetery for me."

After a little while, Sheffler fumbled in the dark for the ash tray and ground out his cigarette. "Look," he said, "I'm sorry for keeping you out here in the cold. How about we go in? I really don't want to be here when a train comes through."

I said okay. Outside there was only the faint stirring of dead leaves in the wind. The car's engine seemed unnaturally loud when Sheffler brought it to life. The headlights threw moving shadows on the pitted concrete as we pulled back onto the road.

I was stiff with the cold when Sheffler dropped me off at the municipal lot. My car was colder still. A mile or two out of Avon, I stopped for coffee at a fast food restaurant that hadn't been open many weeks. It was brilliantly lit, clean, and empty. The stainless steel counter was decorated with orange and black streamers and cardboard cutouts of black cats and witches.

The girl behind the counter was too young to be working so late. Her garish uniform, crisply pressed, made her look like an aide at a cartoon hospital. She acted genuinely pleased to have someone to talk to, and I saw a chance to work on the assignment that had somehow gotten lost during the evening. As she handed me my change, I asked her if she knew the story of the haunted bridge.

"Oh yeah," she said, smiling. "Everybody around here knows that."

She directed a guilty glance toward the kitchen area behind her, but there were no signs of life. "It's supposed to be about this car wreck that happened years and years ago."

I opened my mouth to interrupt her, but she went on without noticing.

"There were these two high school kids who were real in love. They were going to have a baby, and no one knew about it, and they were afraid their parents would make them give the baby up and not see each other anymore. They were real in love, you know."

She checked the kitchen again quickly. "So anyway, one night the two of them got killed by a train at the bridge near here, only it's supposed to be that they did it on purpose so they could be together forever and with the baby, too, you know."

She'd spoken the last part in a hushed whisper, but now her voice dropped even more. "And the real scary part is, when a train goes over the bridge, you can hear the baby crying."

We stood silently for a moment staring at each other over the counter. If my expression was like hers, it was a wide-eyed, half-believing, campfire look, out of place in the light.

I thanked her and started for the door.

When I was halfway there, she called to me. "You know, it's just an old story."

# MAN PERFECTED

The attitude of my editor at the *Star Republic*, E.N. Boxleiter, toward his life was not what you'd call a love affair. It was more that of a man who'd long ago adopted the secret motto "let's get this over with." So I'd never have expected him to take much interest in past lives, his or anyone else's. But when another citizen of our city and my beat, Indianapolis, claimed to have recalled a past life while under hypnosis, Boxleiter surprised me.

"Bring me that pretty balloon," he said to me. "Or the pieces of it."

His somewhat cryptic order meant he wanted the truth behind the past life claim, something for which the news outlet that had broken the story hadn't exactly probed. The outlet in question was Indy's public television station and, more specifically, its weekly program *Underground Indiana*, which presented odd facts about the state, past and present.

The show had a magazine format and usually combined three segments to fill its half hour. So a story on a piece of real Indiana history, the Underground Railroad, say, might run right after one on a man who liked to wear live bees.

I knew the producer and star of the show, Bob Blanchard, and I usually avoided him, as he'd been after me for years. That is, Blanchard had been after my files of strange and unusual stories, stories that had never made it into the pages of the *Star Republic*, even though they were a byproduct of years of cryptic orders from Boxleiter. I'd never opened those files to *Underground Indiana* because I didn't want a past subject of mine squeezed between pieces on bottle cap sculpture and female Elvis impersonators. Luckily for me, Blanchard was nowhere near as tightfisted. When I reached him by phone, he readily recounted his recent coup.

"The guy's legit and then some," he said. "Ex-marine, supervisor at the naval armory, tough as they come. Guy like that claims to have a past life, you don't exactly laugh. Seriously, I was afraid to even smile the whole time I was with him, even though this past life was such a strange match for his latest one. And the way he stumbled onto it—going to some hypnosis clinic to give up smoking—seemed like a sitcom plot. Imagine going out to give up Marlboros and discovering you'd been a black washerwoman. But by the time the interview ended, I'd forgotten all about laughing. It affected me that much.

"And not just me. We've gotten more mail about that

segment than any we've done. It speaks to people, you know, the idea that we have past lives and that they jump across racial and gender boundaries. There's a message in that story. It changed my thinking about the universe, I'll tell you that. Gave me a deeper perspective."

Blanchard then undercut his claim by describing the story he was currently working on, a profile of a soccer-playing llama.

When he finally freed up the phone line, I used it to call the naval armory, itself an oddity in landlocked Indianapolis and an enduring monument to some congressman's political clout. When I reached Craig Kohler, the supervisor with the interesting memories, he readily agreed to an interview. But he put me off for an hour and arranged to meet me at his home.

I used part of that hour to leave a message for Constance Brewster, a friend who taught at Lockerbie University on the city's near north side. Connie was a professor of cultural anthropology, but her interests were far broader. She held a similar view of my interests.

"The things you get into," she said when she returned my call. "Past life regression is way out in left field, even for you. It's been around since the fifties, but like a lot of silly ideas, it had to wait until our education system went completely to pot before it really caught on."

I gathered from that lead-in that Connie was not a believer, but I went through the formality of asking her.

"Do I believe that one's subconscious contains stored memories that a therapist can tap into? Ah, no. I'd have to believe in reincarnation, for starters, and I don't. And I'd have to believe in the value of recovered memories, and we've known for years how dangerous it is to rely on them. They turn out to be products of the subject's imagination or the therapist's conscious prodding or unconscious suggestions.

"The really frustrating thing about past life regression is that we've known from the start that it was a lot of hooey. The very first famous case, in which some woman in Colorado in the fifties remembered being a completely different woman who'd lived in Ireland in the nineteenth century, was exploded by one of your fellow journalists. He found out that the Colorado person had grown up across the street from an old Irish lady. What she was claiming as details of a past life were just memories of the stories her neighbor had told her. That revelation should have strangled the past life regression fad in its crib. Instead, it'll probably outlive the Loch Ness Monster."

Connie told me then that she was late for a lecture, that I owed her a drink, and that she didn't expect to collect until her next incarnation. Before I could laugh politely, she was gone.

By then I was late myself. The Kohler residence was on Forty-eighth Street off Kessler Boulevard. It was an older street that had been added onto to provide access to a new golf course. The Kohler property was on the newer stretch and actually abutted the course. As I pulled up in front of the two-story, brown brick home, a foursome was hitting from a tee next to its driveway.

Craig Kohler, still dressed for work in dark slacks, a white, short-sleeved shirt, and a striped tie complete with tie clip, answered my knock. He was a not particularly tall man of maybe fifty-five, with very square shoulders, a straight back, and a bowler's forearms. His buzz cut—not updated since the marines discharged him—and his narrow eyes and flat nose all gave him a tough-guy air, but that was contradicted by ears so pointed at the top they were almost elfin. And by his current embarrassment.

He brought me inside long enough to introduce me to two women, also middle-aged, his wife, Donna, and his sister, Jackie Hooper. The wife, pretty but nervous, seemed as embarrassed as her husband. The sister was not. She was short and stocky, like Kohler, and her expression dared me to make fun of her baby brother. I deduced the age relationship from a photo on the mantelpiece of the room in which the introductions took place, a black and white of three children. The oldest of the three was a boy who bore only a slight resemblance to the man with two lives. The other boy, who sat on his sister's knee, was a dead ringer for my host, age two. None of the children was smiling.

Kohler then led me out onto a shaded deck, from which we could see the latest group of golfers waiting on the tee.

As soon as we sat down, a yellow Labrador came up from the yard and stretched out at Kohler's feet.

"Sorry for putting you off," Kohler began. "For not talking to you at work, I mean. I'm not ashamed of my story. I want people to know about it. I think it might help some people, the way it's helped me. But ever since that television program, I've taken a lot of kidding down at the armory. You showing up wouldn't have made it die out any faster."

I remarked that a newspaper article wouldn't hurry the process along either.

"I'm not sure any of those knuckleheads can read. Then again, I didn't think they watched public TV. But like I said, I'm not ashamed.

"If you talked to Mr. Blanchard, you know all the background. Donna's been begging me for years to quit smoking. I tried, but nothing took. Finally, she came up with this hypnotism idea. I gave her a raft of crap about it at first."

Here Kohler paused and, to my surprise, blushed. He sat up a little straighter and continued.

"Then I said I'd go. The hypnotist—therapist he calls himself—is a guy named Runacre. His office is on Lafayette Boulevard, down near all the car dealerships. He's a retired navy guy, which settled me down a little. We started off talking about places we'd both been stationed. After ten minutes of that, I told him to bring on the swinging watch.

"He actually just turned down the lights and had me think of a beach near Camp Lejeune, Topsail Beach, which I'd mentioned liking. He asked me to count the waves I was seeing. The next thing I knew, the lights were back on again and Runacre was all excited.

"He said he'd started the session by asking me to think back, way back. Then he asked me when I'd first smoked. According to Runacre, I told him I'd never smoked, that smoking was for fools. And I said it in a . . . different voice."

Here Kohler shifted in his chair, disturbing the Lab, which raised its big head. Kohler patted the dog, and it lay back down.

"Runacre asked me who was speaking. This was while I was still under. I told him my name was Eadie Gill, that I was a sixty-year-old lady from St. Simons, Island, Georgia. That I made my living washing clothes for white folks.

"At that point, Runacre thought to turn on a tape recorder. If he hadn't, I don't think I would have believed a word he told me later. But there was my own voice, only different, talking about St. Simons, a place I've never been, like I knew it by heart. We've checked; everything I told Runacre about the island was true, only it's more built up now and a streetcar line I remembered isn't there anymore.

"By then, my session time was gone. Runacre wanted me to stay and try again. I told him I'd come back."

I asked Kohler why he'd agreed to that. Even now, the memory of that first session made his pointy ears redden.

"I wanted to be sure that Runacre wasn't setting me up, that he hadn't made some suggestion to me before he turned on the tape machine that I'd just parroted back afterward. The only way to check was to bring back my own witness, somebody I trusted. Donna couldn't get off work—she's a teacher's aide—and she suggested my sister, who's retired." He gestured toward the room where we'd left Jackie Hooper.

"One of the best things about this business has been getting back in touch with Jackie. We've lived our lives in the same city but never really talked. We didn't exactly have a happy childhood together. Donna called her once in a while; I never did. But when I needed someone I could trust, Jackie came through.

"We went together to the therapy place the next day, and it was the same routine, with me counting waves and then waking up to Runacre babbling. Jackie was white, but she nodded to me to let me know everything was okay. They played the tape of the session for me. Eadie Gill came on right away, told stories about the island, even sang a song or two I'd never heard before. Runacre couldn't have planted those in my head. On the tape, he doesn't really lead me on. He just asks questions, like 'were you married?' Jackie suggested that one."

Kohler paused abruptly, and I sensed he'd reached some mental hurdle he couldn't bring himself to jump. When he spoke again, it was to sum up.

"Anyway, that's about it. Runacre and Jackie and I did a few more sessions, trying to get back even farther. Eadie Gill was the only one who ever came forward. Bob Blanchard and *Underground Indiana* heard about me through a friend of Runacre's who works at the station. I was sore about that at first, but I decided it might help people to hear about it, the way it's helped me. So I swallowed my pride."

It was the second time he'd spoken of the therapeutic effects of his past life regression. I pressed for more on that, asking Kohler if the discovery that he'd once been an African-American woman had changed his views on race relations.

"No," he said. "If I had any screwy ideas about that, being in the marines all those years straightened me out. It wasn't my views about blacks and whites." He balked at the jump a second longer before plunging over. "It was about men and women.

"Donna and I have been married a lot of years. So many that I started taking her for granted. I may even have abused her. Not physically," he hastened to add, "but there are other ways. I didn't understand that until I listened to the tapes of Eadie Gill.

"She talked about a husband she'd had who was no good. When he wasn't bullying her, he was just plain ignoring her. Either way, he broke her heart. It made me sick to hear it and to realize that I'd treated Donna the same way. I don't understand how I could, given what had happened to me in my other life. It must be that it was buried too deep. That experience couldn't do me any good until Runacre dug it out and put it on tape for me to hear. Me and anyone else who's interested. Like I said, maybe it'll help some other guy who doesn't know how to treat a woman. He might act different if he knows there's a chance he was a woman himself once."

Kohler offered me Runacre's phone number and took me back inside to get it. The two women I'd met earlier had made themselves scarce. I saw again the old photo of Kohler and Hooper and the boy I'd taken for their older brother. I asked about him, not entirely to make conversation.

"Donna put that picture out. I don't know why I even hung on to it. Donna thought Jackie might like it, but I think it gives her the same willies it gives me. The older kid's my brother Fritz. I haven't seen him in forty years. He's a little older than Jackie and me. Five years older than Jackie and ten years older than me."

Kohler added that his brother had retired to Sebring, Florida. Then he showed me out. While he was pumping my arm on the front porch, I asked one more question: Had he quit smoking?

He gave me my first and last glimpse of his smile. "You know, I have. I quit after that very first visit. It's funny, because Runacre never got a chance to make any suggestions about that. I guess knowing that Eadie thought smoking was for fools made me ashamed to do it."

• • •

I tried the number I'd been given for Runacre, first name Donald. The man I reached had a slight southern accent and a mulish attitude. He didn't like it when I told him that Kohler was conducting unsupervised interviews. I thought at first he was afraid of being misrepresented, but his real objection had dollar signs attached. He told me he planned to write a book on the Kohler case. He offered to sell me an exclusive interview on the project—including an opportunity to hear the Eadie Gill tapes—naming a figure that would have given Boxleiter hiccups. I asked for time to think it over.

I decided that a better investment would be a long-distance call to Sebring, Florida, for a chat with the lost sibling, Fritz Kohler. But I didn't have Kohler's number, and a call to directory assistance for Sebring produced no results. Luckily, I had a coworker back at the *Star Republic* named Eric Neuman who could play the Internet like Willie Mays once played center field. I gave him the assignment of finding the older brother and stopped to have lunch at an Irish pub on Fifty-sixth Street.

I wanted to talk to the elder Kohler because I kept thinking back to something my friend the cultural anthropologist had told me about the first famous case of past life regression, namely that the subject had turned out to be remembering a woman she'd known as a child. Craig Kohler seemed sincere, but it could be that he was too young when he'd known the real Eadie Gill to have any conscious memories of her. His brother Fritz, who was ten years older, just might.

The problem with that theory was the sister, Jackie Hooper, who was five years older than her baby brother. If Eadie Gill was a name from the Kohler family's past, why hadn't Hooper recognized it? I chewed over several possible explanations while working through my beef stew. The likeliest answer I came up with was that Hooper had lived apart from her brothers for a time.

I put the speculation aside when Neuman called me back to report success. Before I got any information, though, I had to listen to him patting himself on the back.

"I couldn't find a Fritz Kohler in the entire state of Florida. Then I remembered that some of the Hoosiers who retire down there come back. They want to die up here or they just get sick of the heat. My mother's aunt did that. So I checked closer to home. The man you're looking for is living about an hour south of my desk, down in Nineveh in Brown County."

He gave me Kohler's phone number and his address. I tried the phone number first and got no answer. Then, for lack of a better idea, I used the address. It took me a little south of Nineveh proper, to a lake called Sweetwater. The Kohler cottage was on a finger of the lake, which seemed to be mostly fingers. I didn't bother knocking on the cottage's door. As I'd pulled up, I'd spotted a man in T-shirt and shorts seated on a dock behind the little house, reading a newspaper.

The lanky, gray-haired man, who silently watched my approach, only vaguely resembled the brother and sister I'd interviewed in Indianapolis. In contrast, the Labrador sprawled at his feet was a dead ringer for Craig Kohler's companion. Before I could speculate on a genetic predilection for a certain breed of dog, the man spoke up.

"I've already been tested," he said. I didn't turn and hurry away, so he clarified his message. "My septic system. It's been tested. I've got all the paperwork inside."

I explained who I was, and he grunted. "Sorry, buddy. Our local council's up in the air about the septics. They're trying to push through a new sewer system is what they're doing. You down here to write about that? No? Have a seat and tell me what you are here about."

I started by asking Kohler if he had a brother named Craig and a sister named Jackie.

"I guess I do. I mean, I did, but I haven't spoken to either one of them in decades. Could both be dead for all I know."

I asked if they'd had a falling out.

"Nope. I just don't care much for family. My mother died when I was a kid, just after Craig was born. Not that I blame him. I always blamed my father, a genuine son of a bitch. I couldn't wait to get out of that family or what was left of it, and I never looked back. What's all this got to do with the *Star Republic*?"

I asked if he remembered an Eadie Gill. The expression on his sun-damaged face softened, if only slightly.

"Damn. I haven't thought of her in a long, long time. Sure, I remember her. She was an old woman my dad hired to watch Craig and Jackie after my mom died. A real character was Eadie. Had about three teeth in her head. Used to mumble all the time about my dad's cigars and his drinking and the 'loose women' he went to see. Her other big subject was the place she grew up down south. Never stopped talking, that woman, but she had a soft heart."

Kohler's own heart was somewhat less soft. I guessed that from the sudden edge in his voice when he asked me if I'd come all the way to Sweetwater to talk about a long dead black woman. When I countered by asking him if he ever watched public television, he nearly lost his temper.

"No, I don't watch that left-wing mush. And if you ask me any more questions that don't fit together, I may throw you in the lake."

To save him the effort, I fit my questions together for him by giving him the bare outlines of his brother's appearance on *Underground Indiana*.

"God almighty," Kohler said. "That's old Eadie he's remembering, for sure. She used to tote him around in one of her laundry baskets. She was as close to a mother as the poor kid had."

I asked what had happened to Gill.

"She went back south when Craig was still in diapers or just out of them. I can't remember why. Probably never knew why."

When I suggested that the move might have had something to do with Eadie's husband, Kohler laughed.

"What husband? Eadie Gill was never married. Seems to me she was famous for never marrying. She was always joking about the man she was going to find, and her a bent, old woman with more gums than teeth. At least, I think she was joking."

When I'd recapped Craig Kohler's past life regression for his brother, I hadn't mentioned Craig's memories of an abusive husband or his hope that recovering his connection to Eadie would make him a better man. I didn't mention that part of the story now. Instead, I asked Kohler if his sister would remember Gill.

"Jackie? She might. Seems to me she was Eadie's shadow. But she was only seven or eight when Eadie left, so I couldn't say for sure."

I thanked Kohler for his time and offered to put him in touch with his brother.

"No thanks," he said without reflection. As I stood to go, he emphasized the point. "Don't tell Craig I moved back. Like I said, I'm not much on family. Same goes for Jackie, if you happen to see her."

• • •

Seeing Jackie Hooper was the next item on my agenda. I didn't have to bother Neuman to get her phone number. Indianapolis directory assistance provided it without breaking a sweat. I called Hooper on the drive north, got her answering machine, and told it I wanted to talk to her before

I filed my story. She called back just as Indy's modest skyline came into view and asked me to meet her at a Burger King on Morris Street.

Hooper was there when I arrived, dressed, as she'd been at her brother's house, in a knit shirt that featured a print of a sleeping cat. She was firmly installed in one of the restaurant's plastic booths, looking about as glad to see me as she'd been the first time. She got even less happy when I told her I'd been to visit her older brother.

"I thought Fritz was in Florida," she said. It only took her a second to do the math. "You know everything, I guess."

I guessed I did, too, though it turned out we were both guessing wrong. I started off confidently, though, telling Hooper that Eadie Gill was a past baby-sitter of her brother's, not a past life, that she'd never had a bad husband or any other kind, and that Hooper had known the truth all along. None of that produced more than a sullen stare, so I moved on to more serious charges.

On the drive north from Nineveh, I'd had time to think of a possible motive for Hooper's going along with her brother's delusion. The motive I'd come up with also explained the part of Gill's story Craig Kohler had gotten wrong: her marriage to an emotionally abusive husband. According to Kohler, Jackie Hooper had suggested to Runacre that he ask about a husband. I now believed she had suggested a lot more than that. I was sure she'd conspired with Donna Kohler to emotionally manipulate the hypnotized Craig.

"Of course that's what happened," Hooper said, with more impatience than shame. "I couldn't have been more surprised when Craig asked me to be his witness. You must think we're a strange family, Craig, Fritz, and me. Donna thinks so, and she's right. But we had such a bad time of it after our mother died—our father was a terrible man—that none of us wants to be reminded of it by the sight of the other two.

"Donna's a different matter, being an in-law. I've gotten to like her over the years, and we've stayed in touch. Not that it was easy for me, because a lot of what Donna told me was about Craig treating her worse than his yellow dog. He wasn't as bad as his father, thank God, but he was still a hard man to live with, as cold and sharp-edged as a brick. What else could a man who'd grown up without a mother's love possibly be?

"I spent a whole lot of hours wondering how I could help Donna, short of giving her money for a divorce. I never had a brainstorm. Then she called about this past life regression business. This was after Craig had asked me to be his witness but before I'd gone with him the first time. Craig had been cagey on the phone, but Donna told me everything. As soon as she mentioned Eadie Gill, I saw what must have happened. Donna was really disappointed when I told her. Craig was already off cigarettes just because his "past self" looked down on smoking. And he was even treating Donna better. She asked me not to tell Craig the truth, and I agreed.

"I saw right away how we could improve on what we'd been handed. It all depended on how much Craig actually remembered about Eadie and on how suggestible he was. I vaguely remembered that Eadie hadn't married, but I wasn't sure. If I wasn't, then surely Craig wouldn't be. And I was pretty certain about him being suggestible. The cigarette business told me that. When Runacre got him under and asked about a husband, Craig went right along with it. I knew then we were okay.

"I'd read up on hypnotism before that first session, but I don't pretend to know how it works. Or how the human mind works, for that matter. But I'm convinced that most of what Craig thinks he remembers about Eadie's husband are actually memories of our father, who treated Eadie the way he treated everyone else, badly. I was ready to coach Craig with my own leading questions and the ones I passed on to that simpleton Runacre. It turned out, I didn't have to. Once I'd introduced the idea of a husband, Craig's memories rushed in to fill the void. Memories of his father, as I said, and newer ones of the way he treated Donna.

"He doesn't treat her like that anymore. He's on his way to becoming the man he should have been in the first place."

I asked her what she meant. It seemed to me that Craig Kohler had grown up to be exactly the man he was fated to be, given the father he'd had.

The question made Hooper drop my mental bond rating. "You really don't understand this after all, do you? You think you've exposed a conspiracy of two women, but the real conspiracy's gone right over your head. It's a big one, too. Every woman on the planet's involved, including your own mother. Since the beginning of time, we've been civilizing men, struggling to make every son a little better than his father. Craig almost slipped through because his mother died when he was newborn. If he wasn't quite his father's son, it was because he'd had a surrogate mother, Eadie Gill.

"Donna and I have a chance to finish the work Eadie started, and we're taking it. Not only for Donna's sake, but for Craig's, too. We'll see it through if you'll mind your own business."

I told her I would, but not without feeling that I was letting down my side. The feeling didn't keep me from warning her about Runacre's plan to write a book that might cause another reporter to retrace my steps.

"Leave Runacre to me," Hooper said. "I saw a picture of his wife on his desk. I'll give her a call."

# NOT ALONE IN INDIANA

Hoosiers have been seeing UFOs since before they were called UFOs. This track record may be one of the reasons Steven Spielberg set several crucial scenes of the most ambitious UFO movie of all time, *Close Encounters of the Third Kind*, in Indiana. The state's fascination with the extraterrestrial is far easier to explain than the UFOs' apparent fascination with Indiana. And more difficult still, after a century of unsubstantiated claims, is getting anyone to take a new UFO report seriously. So I was surprised when my editor at the *Indianapolis Star Republic*, E.N. Boxleiter, sent me to rural Everton one July day to interview another witness.

When I asked him what made this sighting different, Boxleiter dismissed me with a question: "Did your grandmother ever lie to you?"

Ethel Hofer was not my grandmother or anyone else's,

as it turned out, but she fit the Madison Avenue image of one perfectly. I found her farm about five miles south of Everton, a town which was little more than a stretch of bad pavement on State Road 1 south of Connersville. The farm was well cared for but not picturesque. The metal-roofed barn and outbuildings crowded the large, unadorned white house, and the straight gravel drive cut the lawn into two equal and empty brown squares.

Ethel Hofer was sitting on her porch as I drove up. In appearance, she continued her farm's theme of plain efficiency. She was a tall woman with large hands that were freckled by age and the sun. Her white hair was pulled straight back from her square face and both her sleeveless house dress and her blue eyes looked washed out from long service. She smiled as I introduced myself and shook my hand.

When I complimented her on the stand of corn that ran to the edge of the yard, she pointed to the house across the road. "Ed Poteet has taken on my land with his so I can keep the place. He's a good friend."

Mrs. Hofer's parlor had a twelve-foot ceiling and a bare wooden floor that creaked as we entered. It was furnished in heavy antiques, including a maroon velvet sofa that barely acknowledged my weight as I sat down. On the mantle, in matching silver frames, were photographs of two men who could only have been father and son. The son was in uniform.

Hofer followed my gaze. "My boy's name is on that wall in Washington," she said. "Dad always talked about going to see it, but we put it off too long.

"Can I get you some tea? I don't have many visitors, so I have to make every one an occasion."

She left for a moment and came back with a large pitcher of iced tea and a plate of oatmeal cookies. Watching her pour the tea, I decided that the impression she had given Boxleiter over the phone had been accurate. It was impossible somehow to imagine her telling a lie.

"Now," she said, "you want to hear about my friends from the sky. First I should tell you that I'm not the kind of person who imagines things. I don't even like things that other people have imagined, like movies and television. I wouldn't have a television in the house. I don't believe in things I can't see or touch. Not anymore. Except for the bonds between people," she added. "Trust and love, I believe in those things.

"I saw the lights last January. My husband, Chester, had passed away in November, so it was a bad time for me. It was snowing that night, and I was sitting here in the parlor feeling sorry for myself. My world had shrunk to a few rooms in this house, and that night it was even smaller, no bigger than the half circle of light cast by the fire. For the first time in my life, I felt truly alone."

She drifted off for a moment, and her pale eyes lost focus. I sat with my tea in one hand and a half-eaten cookie in the other, feeling awkward and a little mad at the editor who'd sent me to Everton. The story I'd come for seemed trivial against the background of the old woman's loneliness.

The widow roused herself with a small shake of her head. "That was when I heard a sound coming from above the house. At first I thought it was an airplane, lost in the storm, but the sound was slower and more rhythmic than an airplane and it seemed to hover, right above my roof. I put on my coat and went out onto the porch. The snow was swirling something furious. I couldn't see as far as the barn. I couldn't see anything but the lights. One was a beam, swinging slowly around the yard. It looked almost like a tube of glass filled with swirling flakes."

As she spoke, she watched a spot on the wall above and behind me. "At the same time, there were little explosions of light, like flash bulbs, only as regular as a clock. They hurt my eyes."

My witness illustrated the flashing lights by rapidly opening and closing her big hands. "I stepped off the porch and looked up into the snow. Up above me, very faint, were red and white lights. Then—in a second, it seemed—they were gone."

She paused to sip her tea. I used the interruption to suggest that what she'd seen might have been a helicopter.

"That's what Ed Poteet said, but I called the sheriff and the airport at Connersville and even the National Guard, and nobody knew anything about a helicopter being lost in that storm.

"So then I went to Connersville to the library to find out for myself. They told me about unidentified flying objects and about all the sightings there have been going way back into history, and they gave me this book."

She picked up a thick volume from the table near her chair and held it out for me to see. The title was *We Are Not Alone*. She had marked various pages in the book with ribbons of different colors that danced as she held the book up. "They lent me their copy of it, I mean. I ordered this one from the bookstore in Laurel so I'd have it handy."

I took the book from her and looked briefly at the marked pages. They described sightings similar to Hofer's, involving mysterious lights in the sky. The last ribboned page contained a passage that had been underlined in pencil, the lines drawn with a ruler. The paragraph related the theory that UFOs visited Earth to check on the status of human development and that actual contact would only be made in an emergency or when sufficient human progress had been attained.

I handed the book back to Hofer, and she held it with both hands.

"That night was the end of a long darkness for me," she said. "After that, I had something to think about besides my troubles. Something to do. I studied my book"—she patted the volume lightly—"until I knew it chapter and verse. And I watched the night sky. You see, I've never believed it was an accident that I saw the lights that night, that they came to my farm out of all the places on Earth. I think there was a purpose to it, but what it was or is I can't say. I hope to know someday."

I asked her what she would do if she never knew, if the lights never came again. The idea didn't seem to bother her.

"It's enough for me to know they're up there," she said. "As for the lights coming back, why they already have. They came one night in May, just when I was beginning to wonder if the whole thing had been a sad dream. I didn't see them myself, worse luck, but my neighbor, Ed Poteet, did and he managed to get a picture. He's quite a photographer and quite clever with gadgets and machines."

When I asked if she had a copy of the photograph, she hesitated before answering.

"Yes, I do," she said, "but Ed asked me to be careful about showing it to anyone. He doesn't believe, you see, as I do that there is a larger pattern to these things and that people should be made aware of them." She smiled. "I think he's afraid that the folks around here will call him a nut."

I assured her that I wouldn't mention the picture to anyone without Ed's permission. She stood up and walked past me to the mantle. The picture was hidden behind the portrait of her son. The print she handed me was a black-and-white five-by-seven. It showed a fuzzy, hubcap-like object festooned with lights. In common with Hofer's visitor, it threw a single shaft of light toward the unseen ground. There was no background detail in the picture, no housetops or trees or stars.

Hofer was standing beside my chair. I stood, too, and thanked her for the interview. On the front porch, she turned and put her hand on my arm. She looked embarrassed, and I decided that she was going to ask me if I believed her story.

Instead, she said, "Have you ever seen strange lights in the sky?"

I told her I hadn't.

She inclined her head toward mine and patted my arm. "Well," she said, "perhaps someday you will."

When I left Hofer, I drove directly to the Poteet farm. It was called "Hilly Acres," according to the brightly painted sign at the end of the drive, and it seemed at least a generation removed from the Hofer farm. The house was sided in blue aluminum and surrounded by flower boxes built of railroad ties. There were several antennas on the roof of the house, and the freshly mown front yard was dominated by a huge black satellite dish, which sat in its own bed of marigolds.

Mrs. Poteet, a plump, dark-featured woman in her forties, answered the door and showed me into a paneled den. "My husband's out to the barn working on the tractor," she said.

While I pretended to examine the stereo, giant television, and other electronic toys that filled the room, she called her husband on an intercom built into the wall.

I'd never met Ed Poteet, of course, but I was prepared to dislike him. Ethel Hofer, as promised, had seemed incapable of guile, but the introduction of a second witness and a photograph opened the possibility that she was the victim of someone else's deceit.

When Poteet appeared and I introduced myself, his reaction seemed to confirm my hunch. He was a bandy-legged man of medium height, somewhere between his wife and Hofer in age. His black hair was cut as tightly as his grass, and his face was ruddy and generously laid out, except for his eyes, which appeared unnaturally small. They seemed to shrink even more when I told him I was researching Hofer's UFO sighting.

"I don't know anything about that," Poteet said. "Except that Ethel is a sweet old soul and nobody should be causing her any trouble."

I agreed with that and told him that she had shown me his picture of the flying saucer. He started to say something and then just shrugged, so I played my last card. I asked him if he'd taken the photo using black-and-white film so it would be easier to retouch.

He took a step toward me, holding his big hands away from his body like a gunfighter ready to draw. "Did you tell *her* that?"

I told him I hadn't.

"I'd throw you out in the road right now if I wasn't sure you'd go blabbing to Ethel. You reporters think you know everything, but you don't know enough not to hurt a lonely old lady."

I asked him if he hadn't hurt her himself by faking the photograph.

Poteet was shocked. "I did that to help her. I've known that woman way over twenty years, and I knew Chester, her husband, and Chet, their boy. I watched her go from a happy soul to near dead. She was smiling when you left her, wasn't she? Wasn't she? Well, what's wrong with that?"

I'd come to accuse Poteet, and I'd somehow ended up in the dock myself. But I wasn't ready to give up. I asked him why he'd given Hofer a phony dream when all she needed was company.

"That's just what I mean," Poteet said. "You think you've got it all figured out, but you don't understand a thing. It isn't company she needs. Why, she was slipping away for years with Chester living right there with her. I've thought sometimes that that was what killed him, seeing her close in on herself year after year without being able to help her."

His gaze had drifted off as he spoke, but now he looked me in the eye again. "Listen," he said, "I'm not going to say another word if it's going to end up in some newspaper. If I can convince you that no harm's been done, can this just be between you and me? Okay then. I'll have to trust you. You could ruin it for her with what you know already.

"It started when Chet got killed in Vietnam. That just about killed his mother, too. Did kill her, in a way. Killed her faith. She'd been a regular at the Baptist church in Everton all her life, a pillar of it, you'd say. When the word came about Chet, we all said, 'Well, she's got her faith,' but we were wrong. She lost it somehow in an instant. She stopped believing that there was anything bigger than her own suffering, any reason for the hard times in this life."

Poteet considered the toes of his boots for a moment and rubbed a hand back and forth over his close-cropped hair. He continued speaking without looking up. "It isn't natural for a human being to live without believing in something. Oh, you may think it is. You may not believe in God or anything else. That's because you come from a city where there's always some light or noise to take your mind from it. But out here there's no noise at night and no lights except for a million stars, and you can get lost in a hurry if you think you're alone.

"The day after she saw her spaceship, Ethel came over to tell us the news. I could see a spark of her old self coming to life. The more she got into this UFO business, the brighter that spark seemed to get. She was looking outside herself again, you see, and outside her own life. Long about May, when nothing more had happened, I saw her start to doubt again, so I made up that photograph. Took it here in the basement.

"I did it, and I'm glad I did. You saw her just now. You tell me whether I hurt her."

Poteet hitched his thumbs in his belt and awaited my

judgment. I looked around the den, at the shelves crowded with audio and video equipment, and wondered if Poteet had tried the city trick of light and noise and found it empty. Then I thought of something Hofer had said: "It's enough for me to know they're there." I told Poteet he'd done the right thing.

He was smiling and friendly as he led me to the door. "This world is bigger than the world we see," he said. "There's more going on in it than we know. Do you believe that?"

When I didn't answer him, he pointed up to the sky. "Those lights, coming out of a snow storm on the night when that lonely old woman was giving up—how can you explain that?"

I told him what I'd told Hofer, that it sounded to me like a helicopter.

Poteet's smile broadened. "I think so, too," he said. "But here's something else. Chester Hofer told me once how his son died. Chet wasn't shot or blown up. He died in a helicopter crash."

He patted my arm as Hofer had. "There's more to this world than we see," he said.

# LYLE PARKHURST'S SECOND COMING

One group a reporter gets to know pretty well is the police. That's especially true of a reporter like me, whose beat is the offbeat. My police aren't the commissioners or even the captains. They're the people in the cars and on the streets, like George Sutphin of the Indianapolis Police Department. He was an older man halfway out the door of the force, who worked traffic control, escorted funerals, or just walked Monument Circle—the Hoosier capitol's geographical center—with the lunchtime crowd. Sutphin was a transplanted Philadelphian. Twenty years in Indiana had not diluted his South Philly delivery, which sounded to my Midwestern ear like New York without the edge. I liked talking with Sutphin, which mostly meant listening to him. So when he called the *Star Republic* one day and asked me to meet him at a Hardee's on Washington Street for coffee, I said okay.

It took us a while to settle in. First, Sutphin had to say hello to everybody in the place. He was a big man, a holdover from the days when most cops were big men, men whose size gave them the calming presence of a horse. He must have escorted a funeral that morning or been planning to work one later, because he was wearing the uniform of a motorcycle cop, including black boots and a bright blue helmet with a vestigial black visor.

I drank my coffee and waited as he worked the room. When he finally sat opposite me, he stalled even more by adding three packets of sugar to his Styrofoam cup, all the time watching me closely while pretending not to.

"You remember Lyle Parkhurst?" he finally asked. "You did a story on him once."

I remembered Parkhurst. He was a street evangelist who worked the Monument Circle area, giving away leaflets and tracts. Parkhurst was as undersized as Sutphin was large, and, like the cop, he was a relocated Easterner, though he'd come to Indiana much later in life. In his first career, Parkhurst had owned a shoe store. He'd had a wife, but no kids. His wife had died about the time Parkhurst was planning to retire, which is the way it often works with plans. It had been a bad time for him, but he'd "found religion" and gotten through it. He had some money put away, more after he sold his store, and nobody in the world.

So he'd begun his second career, spreading the religion that had saved his life.

It was difficult to put a brand on the religion Parkhurst was spreading. He himself called it "Generic Christianity." He'd never been much of a joiner, he told me, so he'd pretty much struck out on his own. He'd bought himself a bag full of stuff, pamphlets and tracts and cards with trick questions like "How would you like to be rich?" on one side and some Bible verse on the other, and started giving the stuff away on the street. He'd found it tough going. Little by little he'd moved west, until finally he'd landed in Indianapolis and found himself accepted. Parkhurst's explanation for his success was that Hoosiers hadn't been overexposed to street religion, making him was something of a novelty. My own theory was that Parkhurst was accepted because he never mixed his preaching with panhandling. You can get along with most people in Indiana if you don't ask them for money.

I told Sutphin what I knew about Lyle Parkhurst, including something I hadn't realized I knew until Sutphin mentioned his name. That was that I hadn't seen Parkhurst around recently. The policeman listened quietly, tasted his coffee, and added another sugar. Then he looked me squarely in the eye.

"Lyle thought he was God," Sutphin said. "I'm not using a figure of speech either. He thought he was God Himself, the Second Person of the Trinity, Jesus Christ. I think that's why he's disappeared."

I got up and refilled my coffee cup at the self-service urn. Then I told Sutphin to give me the story.

• • •

Lyle wasn't always God (said Sutphin). It kind of snuck up on him. When I first met him, he was still just Lyle Parkhurst. It happened one day out on Monument Circle, me meeting him for the first time, I mean. You know how sometimes he'd recite scripture while he handed out his stuff? Or he'd say over and over again, "Keep looking up." I heard him one day, and he sounded like the Delaware Valley to me, so I introduced myself. That was the start. It got so I'd stop to talk with him a couple of times a week. In the winter he'd come here to the Hardee's with me and have a cup of coffee. He told me about his wife and about the shoe business. I told him about being a cop. One day he told me about being Jesus Christ.

We were sitting in this booth right here. I was eating a hamburger sandwich. I mean I'd started to eat one. I never finished it. Lyle looked real sad that day. He asked me to listen to something important. I thought he was going to tell me about his wife, that maybe it was their anniversary or something.

"I'm listening," I told him.

"I figured out something yesterday," Lyle said.

He looked down at the table while he said it. I remember

I could see the bald spot he tried to comb over on the top of his head.

"I had this problem I was thinking about all the time," he said. "It got so I was always thinking about it, whether I knew it or not, no matter what I was doing."

"Unconsciously," I said.

"That's it," he said. "The problem was the Second Coming of Jesus Christ. You ever think about that? It always bothered me that it hasn't happened. All this time has passed and nothing. Is something supposed to happen first? Are things supposed to get better? Worse? I thought about it a lot."

"You'll make yourself sick trying to figure out God," I told him.

That got Lyle excited. "That's the important point," he said. "I think we're supposed to figure out God. I think that's why he gave us brains to begin with."

"And you've got Him figured?" I asked.

"That's what I wanted to tell you," he said. "It happened yesterday morning while I was shaving. I was looking at my face and I started to wonder about Christ's face, what it had looked like. It came to me that He could've looked like anyone. Any guy you pass on the street. He could've looked like me."

"He had a beard," I said.

"And then it hit me," Lyle said. "I think I am Jesus Christ."

I almost repeated the name, you know, as an expression of

surprise. Instead, I asked Lyle, "What do you mean, think? Wouldn't you know?"

"I mean if my thinking is right, I am Jesus Christ," Lyle said. "I'm going to test my idea now."

I told Lyle that I didn't understand.

"I haven't got time for a big explanation," he said. "It's basically like this. We're wrong about the Second Coming. Even the name is wrong. We think of it as something coming down, something outside coming in. Do you know what I'm saying? But we've already had that kind of treatment. The seed's already been sown. The Second Coming's got to be from inside out. You know what I'm saying?"

"No," I said.

"I'm Jesus Christ," Lyle said, "because I want to be Him. No, that's not right. I'm Him because I thought of it. That's what had to happen. Somebody had to wake up one morning and say, 'I can be Jesus Christ. He did it, I can do it. He had no sin, He's taken mine away.' The job's been open for two thousand years. Not following Him or imitating Him. No part-time work. Not being born again as me. Being born again as Him."

"Lyle," I said.

"Jesus," he said.

I told him to keep his voice down. "You're making me nervous. You've cleaned out half the Hardee's already."

"I've got to go now," he said. "I'll tell you more later. If I can."

I tried to stop him. "Let's think about this," I said. "What about all the stuff that's supposed to happen at the end, the angels and the sky opening up?"

He'd left the table by then. I followed him to the door.

"What about this test, Lyle?" I asked him. "You're not going to do anything crazy, are you?"

"Don't worry about me," he said. "Worry about yourself."

He looked right into me when he said it. It scared me. Then he reached up and put his hand on my shoulder.

"I'm pretty much at peace," he said. "But there's still one answer I'm worried about. Even if I turn out to be the Christ, it may not be enough. One Christ may not be enough, I mean."

"How many do you need?" I asked him.

"One for everybody there is," he said. "I mean you and everybody else making up their minds the same way I did."

"That could take a while," I said.

"Two thousand years and counting," he said. "It took two thousand years for some poor schnook from Burlington to have the idea. And now I've passed it on to you. Think about that."

He turned and left me in the vestibule. The last part of what he'd said kind of froze me. It might have been a minute before I followed him. Or tried to. I couldn't find him in the afternoon crowd.

I was worried about Lyle and this test of his. After my shift, I stopped by the shop where he bought all his leaflets and stuff. They gave me his address, which turned out to be an old rooming house on New Jersey Street, so old it only had one toilet per floor. The landlord told me that Lyle had settled with him that morning. I had a look at Lyle's room. All his stuff was gone. It was a miserable little room, just a bed, a chair, a reading lamp, and a washstand with a sink in one corner.

I got down on my hands and knees to look under the bed. I saw a little ball of paper against the wall. It turned out to be a crumpled page from one of Lyle's pamphlets. "Keep looking up" was all it said.

I was standing there, trying to think of my next move, when I got the feeling that there was somebody else in the room. I looked over and saw my reflection in the mirror over the washstand. Lyle's mirror. It startled me. I got out of that room in a hurry.

Now you know everything I know.

• • •

Sutphin and I sat there looking at each other for a moment. I didn't have anything to say, and that seemed to satisfy the policeman. He thanked me for my time and went back out onto the street.

It was one story I never even considered offering to E.N. Boxleiter, my editor at the *Star Republic*. Not even after Sutphin took his retirement and showed up on Monument

Circle one day passing out pamphlets and telling everybody to "keep looking up."

The first time I bumped into him in his new profession, we were both embarrassed. But I wasn't too embarrassed to ask him what he was doing.

"Waiting for Lyle," he told me.

Now we're both waiting.

# ALPHA CENTAURI TO CENTERVILLE

On October 16, 2012, an observatory in Geneva, Switzerland, announced to the world that a planet had been detected in orbit around our sun's nearest neighbor, Alpha Centauri. Alpha Centauri is a binary star in the constellation Centaurus. The new "extrasolar planet" orbits the smaller of the two partner stars, Alpha Centauri B. In keeping with the rules that govern such things, the new world was given the prosaic but functional name Alpha Centauri Bb. At least, that was the new planet's name for everyone on Earth except a woman in Centerville, Indiana, Florence Dean Boand, who had predicted Alpha Centauri Bb's existence years before the Swiss scientists spoke up. She called the planet Marta, and with some authority. She'd been born there, after all.

I heard about Florence Boand from her caregiver, a nurse

named Imogene Crowe. Ms. Crowe phoned the *Indianapolis Star Republic*, the newspaper I oversaw, on the day after the Swiss planet hunters released their news to the world. I'd told my dwindling staff to put a special kind of call directly through to me. I'd described it as the kind of call you hang up on and then wonder about all week. Nurse Crowe's example met that imprecise definition precisely.

"I called the Indy television stations, but none of them was interested," Crowe told me. "I thought about calling the Cincinnati stations, but then I thought of you."

I didn't take offense at the pecking order. Instead, I asked Crowe about her relationship with Florence Boand.

"I'm Ms. Boand's daytime caregiver. I'm a retired nurse—semiretired, I should say. Semiretirement is as much as a person can hope for these days. I used to work for Methodist Hospital in Indy, so I read your paper every day I had the time. Never got one finished, though. Nowadays, when I have nothing but time, the papers are all so thin you can't wrap up a good-sized fish in one. That's life, I guess.

"Ms. Boand was hurt in an auto accident. She suffered a traumatic brain injury, poor soul, and can't care for herself. Her sister's here at night, and I'm here days. Ms. Boand was a teacher. So was her husband, who was killed in the same awful wreck. Ms. Boand is still smart, but her brain is all jumbled up. That truck that crossed the centerline and hit her just jumbled everything in her head.

"She has good days, though. On those, she sometimes

tells me about Marta, the planet she came from. She told me once that it had a sun we Earth people call Alpha Centauri. So when I heard about Alpha Centauri on the news, about the planet they found right where Ms. Boand said it would be, I thought I should tell someone. About Marta, I mean. Do you think we should call those people, the ones from Marta, I mean, Martians?"

Resisting the urge to suggest that the people from Mars might sue, I asked if I might come by to meet Ms. Boand. Nurse Crowe thought that would be fine, as her charge was having an especially good day.

Once upon a time, I would have been sent to speak to Florence Boand by E.N. Boxleiter, my editor and mentor, who'd had a weakness for an offbeat story and had recognized in me a kindred spirit. But Boxleiter had died in harness shortly after the *Star Republic* had been purchased by a "media conglomerate," without getting to enjoy even a semiretirement. That was life, as Nurse Crowe had observed. She'd also observed that the *Star Republic* was getting smaller. She'd been referring to the number of pages per issue, but it was even truer of the newsroom head count. We were well on our way along the transition from real newspaper to repackager of others people's content. I was reluctantly overseeing that transition, but every once in a while, I escaped the office to go in search of a Boxleiter story. For old times' sake.

My current search took me east on U.S. 40. Taking I-70 to

Centerville would have been faster, but the fall colors were better seen from 40, the old National Road and the country's first interstate highway. Once clear of Indy's suburbs, the road was a time machine, a trip past towns designed to service a western migration long since ended, the towns set apart at an almost uniform distance: the distance a team of oxen could pull a covered wagon in a single day.

Centerville, which I reached in a leisurely hour and a half, was one of those old wagon stops, though it had reinvented itself several times, most recently as an antiquing center, complete with small shops and a sprawling antique mall. Ms. Boand's house—or rather, the home of her sister, Cecilia Dean—was very near the mall, on the road that connected Centerville with I-70. The house itself was no antique, being a well-kept ranch whose only distinguishing feature was a long wheelchair ramp leading to the front door.

The user of that ramp awaited me in the home's living room. I was admitted by Nurse Crowe, who was older than her voice had suggested: gray and stooped, but with a brisk and businesslike step. Florence Dean Boand was likewise a surprise. Based on what I'd been told, I'd expected someone physically damaged, perhaps with some outward sign of the blow that had "jumbled everything in her head." I saw no such mark or scar, despite her very short brown hair. Boand, in a gray polo shirt and tan slacks, was seated in a wheelchair, but she sat erect. She was perhaps fifty and very thin, with paper-dry skin and large, green eyes. The eyes were the only outward sign of her condition other than the chair. That is, her left eye was. Though it moved in perfect concert with her right eye—both following me as I entered the room and seated myself before her—it somehow lacked all light and life.

Nurse Crowe had covered my entrance with a steady patter on the subject of Marta and the *Star Republic*'s interest in it. Before I could confirm or deny that interest, Boand said, "Alpha Centauri is four point three seven light years from Earth."

Crowe, seated beside her charge, beamed proudly, and I took the opening I'd been given, asking Boand how she'd managed to cross that long void.

She frowned in concentration and then said, "We saw deer that day in the park."

The response got Crowe frowning, too. "There's the jumble I was talking about. Those deer are always popping up. They must've been wonderful deer." She patted Boand's hand. "He's asking how you got here from Marta, honey."

"We were sent here in exile. Raymond and me. As a punishment."

"Raymond was her husband," Crowe supplied. "A punishment for what, honey?"

"Disobedience. We were sent to live with lesser beings. To be lesser beings ourselves. It was in the summer. . ."

"When you first came here from Marta?" Crowe prompted.

"No. When we saw the deer."

While Crowe shook her head, I asked what Marta was like. This was for purposes of comparison with Alpha Centauri Bb. According to the Swiss, the planet was a little bigger than Earth, but with a surface many times hotter. Twelve hundred degrees Celsius, in fact.

"It was a paradise," Boand said. "A perfect paradise we could never get back to. Never really even remember clearly." She paused, concentrating. "Yes, it was summertime when we were in Tennessee."

"We're back to the deer," Crowe said with a sigh.

Somewhere in the back of the house, a kettle was working itself up to whistle. "Would you like some tea?" the caregiver asked me. "We always have tea about this time. I'll be right back."

As soon as she'd gone, I decided to play a hunch. If those deer always interrupted a discussion of Marta, perhaps they weren't interruptions at all. Perhaps they were an important preamble that Crowe kept interrupting unknowingly. So I asked Boand about them.

At once, her faltering voice became steadier. "We were at a state park in Tennessee. Taking a walk on a trail by a lake. Two deer stepped out onto the trail ahead of us, a doe and a buck. They stood there for a second, the doe with her head down and the buck staring right at us. Then they bounded off.

"We joked about them being lovers, like us. Raymond said

they could even be resurrected lovers, a human couple reincarnated as lesser beings. He said they wouldn't care about being deer now and not people, because they were together. He said we would be the same way if it happened to us: happy forever just because we were together.

"The idea made him smile, but it bothered me. . ."

It bothered Boand still, to judge by her troubled expression. She shook her head and said, "Alpha Centauri is four point three seven light years from Earth."

I nodded in agreement and then asked her why Raymond's romantic notion of the reincarnated lovers had troubled her so. I asked without much hope, but Boand picked up the earlier strand of thought almost as though she'd never let it go.

"I felt a terrible sadness whenever I thought of those deer. It wouldn't go away. The sadness was like a memory I could only feel, never recall. When Raymond died, the feeling grew worse and worse. I thought of those deer many times. We saw them in Tennessee."

I nodded again, afraid Boand had gotten stuck in some kind of loop. She hadn't.

"Why had their story made me so sad *before* I lost Raymond? All at once, it came to me. It had to be that Raymond had been right without knowing it. We had been condemned, just we two, to live as lesser beings, among lesser beings. When I realized that, everything made sense, everything I'd felt since that day in Tennessee. Everything I'd felt since the accident."

A bit of Motown started playing in the background, the Marvin Gaye hit "I Heard it Through the Grapevine." I realized, when Gaye abruptly stopped and Crowe began speaking, that it had been a cell phone's ringtone. Crowe's nervous repetition of "yes" stopped Boand cold. To get her going again, I reminded her of a detail she'd mentioned earlier. It was that she and her husband had been exiled for "disobedience."

"Because we were lovers and we were forbidden to be lovers. Because one of us was highborn, and the other was a commoner. Because Raymond was highborn, and I wasn't. I realized that all at once, too, but not until after Raymond was gone. When he'd had that thought about the reincarnated deer, he hadn't been making up a story; he'd been close to remembering the truth about Marta. We both had been. And the truth is we were cast out of the garden, like your Adam and Eve, sent here to Earth to live with beings as far beneath us as deer are beneath them. And now I'm here alone."

Crowe entered at a trot, not carrying a tea tray. I considered that an ominous sign, and it was.

"That was Ms. Dean, Ms. Boand's sister. She's on her way home. One of the neighbors phoned her at work about your car being in the drive. Ms. Dean is very unhappy. You have to go now, please. I can't afford to lose this job."

Crowe was very agitated, and the woman in the wheelchair was picking up the vibe and amplifying it, holding her hands to her jumbled head in sympathetic distress. I thanked them both for their time and told them that everything would be all right, though Crowe undercut the calming tone I tried to hit by opening the front door with some urgency in the middle of my speech.

Once outside, I had to decide whether I would actually go or if I'd put Crowe's position at risk by waiting to interview Cecilia Dean. That ethical dilemma was resolved for me by Dean's arrival and by the fact that she bottled up my car in the narrow drive by parking hers behind it.

A moment later, I was grateful for my gray hairs, as they made an assault on my person slightly less likely. Only slightly, because Dean, a female linebacker wearing a muted pantsuit and a fiery complexion, was, as Crowe had understated it, very unhappy.

Dean demanded to know who I was and what I wanted. I was pretty sure Crowe had already answered both questions for me. Otherwise, Crowe wouldn't have been afraid for her job, and Dean's blood pressure would have been less readable in her cheeks. Nevertheless, I went through the motions of replying, even going so far as to produce my press card. Not the shiny, plastic one the media conglomerate had provided, but the old, cardstock one Boxleiter had given me so many years before. It had carried me through more than one awkward encounter like this. More than a score of them.

I explained my interest in her sister's story, tying it to the recent announcement of Alpha Centauri Bb.

"How can you think of making a laughing stock of a poor soul like that, who doesn't even know what day of the week it is?"

I pointed out that Boand knew the distance to the nearest star.

"She was a science teacher," Dean replied with exasperation. "She can tell you the boiling point of mercury. That's enough to fool someone like Imogene Crowe. She never knew Florence when she was whole. She doesn't know how much of Florence is gone."

I asked Dean if she knew the story of the deer.

"I should. I've heard it a thousand times. I could tell you what it really means, but you'd only use the truth to mock my sister."

I promised her I wouldn't and that no part of her sister's story would appear in the pages of the *Star Republic* without Dean's permission. It was a promise that a person familiar with reporters wouldn't put much faith in. But I'd learned over the years that a certain kind of person would accept it: a person being crushed by the weight of an untold story.

Sure enough, after a token hesitation, Dean started in. While she talked, her complexion lightened a shade or two. And her manner softened.

"Florence and Raymond met in college. Earlham, over in Richmond. Ray came from money and Flo was a scholarship student. His family would never have let him marry so far beneath the precious Boands, except that she got pregnant. Even so, they all but cut Ray off. He and Flo got by on small-town teachers' salaries.

"That's the fall from grace Flo feels but can't quite remember. That's how she got to be from Alpha Centauri."

I asked Dean what had happened to the child.

"She died on the day she was born. So Ray had spit out his silver spoon for nothing. And Flo was left with nothing but the feeling that she'd ruined his life. And that was all *before* the truck hit them. It's no wonder she became an outcast from another solar system. Her life on Earth was so much sadder."

I apologized again for intruding and tried to put in a good word for Crowe. Dean cut my endorsement short.

"I'm not going to fire her. I can't afford anyone better."

She said that with her hand on the door handle of her car. Though I was still anxious to have my escape route cleared, I also had another question. Raymond Boand had been a vaguely drawn but positive character in his widow's version of events. His sister-in-law's story suggested a darker shading. I reminded Dean that it was Raymond who had first joked to his wife about being reincarnated as a lesser being. I asked Dean if she thought he'd done that to point up his continuing devotion to Florence or to remind his wife of all he'd given up for her.

Dean's barometric cheeks flashed red again. "Go ask him yourself."

Dean moved her car then, pointedly blocking the main road until I backed out myself. Before I did, I looked at the house one last time and silently wished Nurse Crowe the best of Hoosier luck. Dean was stopping traffic in the northbound lane for me, assuming that I'd head up to I-70 and then turn west for Indy. I took her suggestion, being less interested now in slow, bucolic drives.

I'd only gone half a mile north when I saw an old iron arch. It spanned a side road and held aloft rusted letters that spelled out "Centerville Cemetery." Dean's parting suggestion, that I ask Raymond Boand my last question, now made sense. At the time, I'd thought she'd been trying to say "go to hell" without actually saying it. Now I knew she'd meant that I'd be passing Boand's grave and could stop and ask it my last question, for all the good that would do me.

Though I was sure it would do me no good at all, I turned in under the arch and parked. I'd found answers in cemeteries before, but only when there'd been living people around to supply them. There were no such people in the Centerville Cemetery, no groundskeepers and no mourners. Not even any fall foliage enthusiasts, though the northern edge of the property had as striking a line of sweet gums as I'd seen anywhere, each tree a tower of purple, yellow, and red leaves. Beyond that display of beauty, the traffic on the interstate passed in an endless and uncaring procession.

I started a procession of my own, on foot, climbing the near side of the hill the rows of graves crossed and then descending the far side. I repeated the trek over and over, looking for Raymond Boand's headstone.

Eventually, I found it. And I found an answer as well. Not the answer to the question I'd posed to Dean. The low gray stone couldn't tell me whether the man resting beneath it had been expressing his devotion or his regret when he'd made the remark about the deer that now haunted his widow. What I found was another piece to a puzzle as jumbled as Florence Boand's mind. The headstone told me that Raymond Boand wasn't the only person buried there. As I should have guessed, his infant daughter rested beside him.

In addition to the single date that represented her entire life, the marker bore her name. It was Marta.

# About the Author

Terence Faherty is the author of the first *Star Republic* story collection, *Tales of the Star Republic*, as well as the Edgar-nominated Owen Keane series, which follows the adventures of a failed seminarian turned metaphysical detective, the Shamus-winning Scott Elliott private eye series, which is set in the golden age of Hollywood, and the standalone Irish mystery *The Quiet Woman*. His short fiction has won the Macavity Award from Mystery Readers International.

Terry lives in Indianapolis, Indiana, with his wife Jan.